EBURY PRESS
PRESS 9 FOR A CRIME

Shailendra Jha is the creator and co-writer of the highly acclaimed Disney+ Hotstar (now JioHotstar) series *Grahan*. He is a recipient of the prestigious Screenwriters Association Award. His writing has earned him multiple nominations for various awards, including the Filmfare OTT Awards.

His short film *Tumhare Bina* has been screened at several international film festivals, including the Bengaluru International Short Film Festival and the South Asian Short Film Festival.

In the news industry, Jha launched and led India's first speed news channel, Tez. He headed the output team during his tenure at India's leading news channel Aaj Tak. He left the TV Today Network as an executive editor and transitioned into the entertainment world, working with Star India, where he held key roles, including programming head, commissioning head and head of branded content.

He continues to create stories independently as a writer, director, show-runner and creative consultant, with a focus on developing web series and films.

ADVANCE PRAISE FOR THE BOOK

'Fast, fierce and frighteningly believable. This is the kind of thriller that keeps you turning pages—and then keeps you up at night thinking about the world we live in'—**Imtiaz Ali, film-maker**

'Some books entertain and some scare you. This one does both—and leaves you checking if your camera is still on. It's funny, sharp and just real enough to make you nervous—this book knows exactly where today's scams hit hardest'—**Divya Prakash Dubey, author and screenwriter**

'Tense, timely and terrifying, Shailendra Jha delivers a modern crime classic with a beating human heart. This is a fearless, fast-paced story that grips you from page one. *Press 9 for a Crime* is fiction rooted in frightening reality'—**Satya Vyas, author**

'A dreadfully real account of a crime which is also a cautionary tale in this digitally dependent world of ours. The power of Jha's writing lies in his penchant for mundane but important details and in his ease with language. *Press 9 for a Crime* is not just that unputdownable racy crime novel you will safely tuck away in your bookshelf, it's a book you will share with friends and family, who need to be aware of just how vulnerable we all are'—**Anu Singh Choudhary, writer and film-maker**

Press 9 for a Crime

SHAILENDRA JHA

An imprint of Penguin Random House

EBURY PRESS

Ebury Press is an imprint of the Penguin Random House group of companies whose addresses can be found at global.penguinrandomhouse.com

Published by Penguin Random House India Pvt. Ltd
4th Floor, Capital Tower 1, MG Road,
Gurugram 122 002, Haryana, India

First published in Ebury Press by Penguin Random House India 2025

Copyright © Shailendra Jha 2025

All rights reserved

10 9 8 7 6 5 4 3 2 1

This is a work of fiction. Names, characters, places and incidents are either the product of the author's imagination or are used fictitiously, and any resemblance to any actual person, living or dead, events or locales is entirely coincidental.

Please note that no part of this book may be used or reproduced in any manner for the purpose of training artificial intelligence technologies or systems.

ISBN 9780143476146

Typeset in Goudy Old Style by MAP Systems, Bengaluru, India
Printed at Replika Press Pvt. Ltd, India

This book is sold subject to the condition that it shall not, by way of trade or otherwise, be lent, resold, hired out or otherwise circulated without the publisher's prior consent in any form of binding or cover other than that in which it is published and without a similar condition including this condition being imposed on the subsequent purchaser.

www.penguin.co.in

For Ma and Babu,
you lived simple lives with extraordinary love,
and found joy in your children's joys.
You stood behind every step I took,
even when it was difficult for you.
I wish you could have held this book.
I remember, and I miss you.

Prologue

Delhi shrugged off its morning haze that mid-March day. The sky was bright after months of deadly smog. And the mood was equally bright in autorickshaw driver Anand Kumar's house in the cramped lanes of east Delhi's Mandawali. The family's eldest son, Atul, was leaving for Bangkok, trading his data entry job for what promised to be a lucrative position abroad.

Aseem leaned against the wall, his gym-trained frame tense as he watched his older brother pack. At twenty-four, the youngest of the four siblings had his own dreams—dreams that required money his father wouldn't provide. His eyes darted between Atul's suitcase and their father, weighing his next words.

'Bhaiya,' he finally decided to not hold it back, 'about starting my own gym that I mentioned—the opportunity will not last long. So, try to send me the money quickly.'

'Aseem!' Their father Anand's sharp tone rang through the room. 'Let your brother breathe. He hasn't even left yet.'

'I have to ask him because you won't help me,' Aseem mumbled.

'With what money?' Anand's celebratory mood cracked. 'Should I sell myself?'

'It's fine, papa.' Atul stepped in, ever the mediator. 'I'll save what I can and send it to you. Use it the way you think is right.'

Aseem's face fell. He knew he was not going to get the money from his father, for whom the priority was his sister Radhika's marriage. Just then, Radhika entered the already crowded small living room, dressed for her job at a construction company. At twenty-eight, she couldn't help but feel frustrated. Her brother Atul, only a year older, seemed to be on the path to a secure future, while she was stuck in a job she hated. To make things worse, the family's financial struggles had put her marriage prospects on hold indefinitely.

'Have you kept any thekua for me?' Radhika asked her mother, who was busy packing homemade sweets and snacks with Radhika's younger sister Tulika's help.

'I'll make it for you later. Where am I going?' Tulsi replied, wrapping another package.

'Sure.' Radhika's lips tightened. 'The sons always come first.'

'It's not like that, didi.' Tulika said gently. 'Atul bhaiya will be living by himself in a foreign country. He needs these.'

Anand, his auto parked outside ready to take them on their way, beamed at his eldest son. 'Beta, make sure you've got everything.'

'Don't worry, papa.' Atul looked up from his methodical packing. 'I've checked everything twice.'

Aseem snatched up his helmet. 'I should go. Have a safe flight.' He strode out of the house to his parked bike, but Atul followed.

'Is this how you want me to remember you? Sulking?'

'Absolutely.' Aseem's grin broke through. 'Let it haunt you into sending that money faster.'

'Rascal,' Atul said, smiling.

The brothers embraced.

'Everything will work out,' Atul promised, ruffling his younger brother's hair. 'Just be patient.'

'I'll try.' Aseem kicked his bike to life. 'Take care. And try to have some fun. Boring man.'

Atul tried to kick him, but Aseem rode away with a final wave, unaware of the gathering storm.

***

Just two kilometres away, in a modest flat in Mayur Vihar Phase 1, former journalist Nitesh Mishra stared at his laptop's blank screen. Six months of unemployment had driven him to attempt writing a novel, but the words refused to come. His phone buzzed—an unknown number. He would have ignored it, but the hope that it could be regarding a job lead made him answer the call.

Nitesh could not immediately make out whether it was a recorded voice or someone was on the call with him. The sound crackled, distant and unclear, first in Hindi then in English. There was something about pressing 9 for information regarding a failed delivery. *What delivery could this be?* He pressed 9.

'Is this Nitesh Mishra?' a male voice asked, suddenly crystal clear.

'Speaking,' Nitesh replied.

'Is this your address? B 109, Samachar Mitra Apartment, Mayur Vihar Phase 1, Delhi 110091.'

'Yes.'

'And this mobile number 9811404xxx is yours too?'

'You called this number; I am speaking on this number. Whose will it be if not mine?' Nitesh snapped, the frustrations of his recent failures getting the better of him. Outside, the pressure cooker whistled in the kitchen and his wife Madhu's footsteps hurried across the floor.

'Why can't you people just get to the point?' Nitesh continued.

The caller abruptly switched to Marathi, his tone becoming more official.

'*Mi Vaibhav Desai bolte*, senior inspector, Mumbai police crime branch. *Tumcha virudh ekat complaint aahe.*'

A heavy silence followed.

Nitesh's heart skipped a beat. Though he didn't understand Marathi, the words 'police', 'crime branch' and 'complaint' didn't need any translation. His mouth went dry as memories of six months ago flooded back—the police raid at his office, being questioned, the fear in everyone's eyes.

'Sir, can you speak in Hindi or English please?' His voice came out with difficulty, his fingers now gripping the edge of his desk.

'Mr Nitesh Mishra, an FIR has been filed against you.' The voice carried the weight of authority, confirming the dread that had been building in Nitesh's stomach.

'What? What FIR? Why?' His voice cracked slightly.

'For facilitating transfer and sale of contraband goods. We have been informed by the customs department that they have seized a courier from Thailand containing banned drugs that mentions your address and phone number.'

The room seemed to spin. 'What . . . ? Drugs . . . I haven't ordered anything from Thailand!' The memory of the police questioning him and his colleagues flashed through his mind again, making his pulse race faster.

'It has your address and your phone number. Both of which you have confirmed.'

'But I haven't ordered . . . I haven't ordered anything even from Amazon in the last month!' Sweat beaded on his forehead despite the cool morning air from the window.

'I am sending you a copy of the FIR. You need to come to the Oshiwara Police Station in Andheri West, Mumbai within working hours today.'

'One minute, sir . . . I cannot come at such short notice. I live in Delhi . . . you have the address.' His voice trembled slightly as he mentally calculated the time it would take and the price of tickets for same day Delhi–Mumbai flights.

'You need to answer some questions, for us to file a report.'

'Can I not do this somewhere in Delhi?'

'Are you not taking this seriously? If the complaint is in Mumbai, you have to come to Mumbai—either of your own will or we will bring you.' The caller's tone turned harsh, making Nitesh flinch.

Silence filled the room, broken only by the sound of his rapid breathing. The morning sun streaming through his window suddenly felt hotter.

After what seemed like an eternity, the caller spoke again, his voice now surprisingly sympathetic.

'Maybe your address and number has been misused. But we have to go through the process since a complaint has been filed. We are just doing our duty. You understand, no?'

'Yes . . . Yes, sir.'

'There is a way to complete the process online.' The caller continued in his sympathetic tone. 'But for that, I will have to bring in a senior officer from the crime branch and you have to be on camera till the process is completed. Do you want to opt for online questioning?'

'Yes . . . yes. I will do this online.' Nitesh's shoulders sagged with sudden relief, though anxiety still churned in his stomach.

'I am sending you a link. We will proceed on a video call,' The voice instructed.

* * *

Two lives. Two kilometres apart. Neither knew the other existed, yet unseen forces were drawing them into the same dark web. Such is life's cruel irony—we're all experts at spotting trouble, till we are not.

One

1

THE METALLIC CLANG OF WEIGHTS and whir of treadmills filtered through as Aseem stepped into the locker room. The familiar mix of sweat, deodorant and cheap room freshener filled his nostrils. He caught his reflection in the full-length mirror and ran his fingers through his hair, carefully restyling the areas that had gone damp and flat from wearing a helmet. The old wall clock showed he had fifteen minutes before his shift started.

Taking off his T-shirt, he reached for the trainer's uniform. The mirror reflected a fit and lean physique, not overly muscular. It was the kind of build that made clothes fall nicely.

Aseem had tried modelling, thinking he could break into fashion and eventually movies. Reality proved very different. He only managed catalogue shoots for a few local merchants and ended up as the face of a juice centre. That singular achievement had become something of a family joke, one his siblings never let him forget.

Aseem believed there had to be an easier way to make money than slogging for someone else. But his get-rich-quick schemes always ended badly. However, the failures had not dented his confidence. He resented that his father didn't support his ideas. More than anything, Aseem was determined to prove him wrong.

The locker room door creaked open and Ravi's muscular frame appeared. Unlike Aseem's lean build, Ravi looked like he could bench press a car—exactly the kind of trainer clients expected to see.

'Hey, Aseem! Got a minute?'

'Sure, what's up?' Aseem said, pulling on his training pants.

Ravi stepped closer, his training shoes squeaking against the floor. 'So, where are we with the money?' His voice had dropped to a hushed tone.

Aseem suddenly got interested in arranging his locker contents. 'I'm working on it, bro. It's not easy to come up with that kind of cash.'

'I get it, but you sold me on this idea!' Ravi spoke with some annoyance, his arms crossed. 'We need to start now to get it running by August, September. Most sign-ups happen after festivals or before weddings.'

They shared a knowing laugh.

'How much have you saved so far?' Ravi asked.

'Don't worry,' Aseem said, unconsciously running a hand through his hair—a nervous habit from childhood. 'My brother Atul just landed a great job in Bangkok. He'll help. I just need more time.' The words tasted hollow even as he said them.

Ravi squeezed his shoulder. 'Figure it out, buddy. This is your chance to be the boss, just what you want.'

As Ravi walked away, his footsteps echoing, Aseem called out, 'Hey, what do you call a gym trainer who can't do push-ups?'

Ravi turned, his eyebrows raised. 'What?'

'A push-over!' Aseem grinned.

Ravi groaned and waved him off, but left the tiny room smiling.

Aseem looked at his nearly empty wallet before putting it in the locker and slumped onto a bench. Five minutes before his shift started. He pulled out his phone and began scrolling mindlessly through social media, past perfectly filtered lives and success stories that made his own dreams seem further away.

His phone buzzed, Soni's name lighting up the screen with a heart emoji she had added herself.

'*Bol meri* Soni,' Aseem answered, his voice automatically softening.

'Hi *mera* hottie! At the gym?' Her voice carried its usual playful lilt.

'*Na! Tere dil mein!* I am always in your heart.' He found himself smiling, the tension of a few minutes ago melting away.

'Cheezy *haan*! Love you for that! Wanna go for a movie?'

Aseem hesitated, thinking of his empty wallet. 'I don't know. I'm not really in the mood . . . Atul went today,' He said, trying to find a convincing excuse.

'Oh,' she said, disappointment clear in her voice. Then, more softly, 'How about coming to my house tonight?'

'To your house?' His heart rate picked up. 'Are you mad? *Tera baap—*'

'*Nahi hai,*' Soni interrupted, her voice dropping to a whisper that sent shivers down his spine. 'My parents are out. We will have the place to ourselves.'

Aseem sat up straighter, suddenly very alert. 'Oh yeah? What time?'

'What happened to your sad mood?' Soni teased and he could picture her pretty smiling face. 'You don't have to come if you don't want to.'

'No, no! I want to!' All his troubles had evaporated.

Soni giggled, the possibilities in that sound creating sensations in Aseem's whole body.

'How about ten?' Soni was asking.

'O . . . yes . . . yes!' Aseem's words fell over each-other.

'Perfect. See you then!'

As he hung up, a grin spread across his face. Outside the chatter and the clink of weights created the familiar symphony. He stood up, stretched, and headed out to crush his shift, his steps lighter than they had been all morning. Maybe the day wasn't a total bust after all.

2

Anand Kumar expertly weaved his auto through the office hour traffic. He bowed his head slightly as they crossed the Bhairon Baba temple—believed to have been established by the Pandavas—near Purana Qila. In the backseat, Atul and Tulika folded their hands. Anand had insisted on dropping Atul, and Tulika had joined them for part of the ride before heading to the university.

Atul sat balancing a laptop bag on his knees. His new suitcase, bought for this journey, rested awkwardly in the cramped space between their feet. A smaller shoulder bag was wedged tightly into the narrow alcove behind the driver's seat.

The sun was climbing higher in the sky, yet the breeze that passed through the open sides of the rickshaw still carried a hint of winter and made it pleasant.

Anand's gaze was fixed on the road ahead, but his mind was drifting to old memories. He had come to this overwhelming city twenty-four years ago with his wife and two little kids. Most of his ancestral land had been lost to a river. The Kamla river flooded every year but that particular year it changed its course and Anand's life. Back then, survival was his only goal. Now, his son was going abroad.

'Papa, drop me here.' Tulika's voice cut through Anand's reverie. They were on the other side of the road from the Central Secretariat metro station.

Anand's fingers found the indicator switch by muscle memory as he eased the auto toward the curb, watching in the side mirror as his daughter gathered her things.

'*Mann laga ke padhna*, okay?' Anand said with the involuntary ease of the parent who had raised four children.

'Yes, papa.' Tulika smiled. 'Have a safe flight, bhaiya. Call us when you reach.'

'I will. You focus on your preparation, don't think too much about last year.' Atul's face showed affection for his little sister.

Anand touched the photo of Hanuman ji placed above the steering wheel with his right hand. *Keep her safe.*

Every morning before leaving home, Anand followed a simple ritual. He bowed in front of the small wooden shelf adorned with pictures of various deities, reached for the keys kept before them and uttered the same prayer: *O God! Bless my family. Keep the girls safe and the boys out of trouble.*

Simple words, that carried the weight of a father's love and worry. In today's world, it could be seen as patriarchal. But no one except Tulsi knew and she didn't have a problem.

As they approached their destination, Anand felt a swell of pride. Atul, his firstborn, off to Bangkok for a promising job. Tulika, diligently preparing for her civil service exams. Even Radhika, though still unmarried, had found steady work with a big builder.

But then there was Aseem.

Anand's grip on the steering wheel tightened involuntarily. The youngest, he was a dreamer. Always with grand plans, always reaching for the stars without considering the ground beneath his feet.

'Papa, I've been thinking,' Atul's voice rose above the rumble of the auto. 'I should be able to save close to one lakh rupees every month. That way in six months, we should have enough to take care of Radhika's marriage expenses.'

Anand's eyes misted over, touched by his son's thoughtfulness. He cleared his throat, trying to keep his voice even. 'You have always been responsible, beta. But make sure you're comfortable. Don't worry too much about home. Your old man can still work hard and provide for the family.'

Atul nodded, a determined look in his eyes. 'I know, papa. But it's time I shouldered more responsibility and you take it little easy.'

They had reached the Airport Express metro station at Dhaula Kuan. Anand would have liked to drop his son right at the departure terminal of the Delhi airport, but autos were not allowed there.

Anand pulled over, his throat tightening as he watched Atul gather his bags—a father's pride warring with a parent's instinctive fear of separation. Atul climbed out and turned back with that responsible eldest-son expression Anand knew so well. 'Once Radhika's marriage is taken care of, I can start sending money for Aseem.'

'Let him first understand the value of hard-earned money. Otherwise he will continue to take it easy and lose it all,' Anand counselled.

He placed his hand on Atul's head as his son bowed down to touch his feet and then pulled him in a tight embrace.

'Take care of your health. Do not worry too much about home.'

They looked at each other with moist eyes for a moment before the father added, 'Don't start smoking or drinking.'

'I won't, papa. You don't worry,' Atul replied with a smile.

The words from the daily prayer echoed in Anand's mind. *Keep him out of trouble.*

'Take care, beta,' Anand murmured, his hand lingering on Atul's shoulder before letting go. He stood rooted to the spot, watching his firstborn navigate through the crowd and go inside the station. Until he could no longer see him. A cold knot formed in his stomach as he questioned himself: *Was he doing the right thing, letting his son venture so far into unknown lands?*

3

Nitesh's hands trembled as he positioned his laptop on the study table. The video chat window was open, displaying a logo that had 'Mumbai Police' and 'Crime Branch' written in it. His throat felt dry.

The caller's face replaced the logo. He was in police uniform.

'Mr Mishra, as I mentioned earlier, it's possible someone used your details. However, since the package is in your name, the FIR stands against you.' His tone was matter-of-fact, devoid of empathy. 'We have a senior officer joining us with additional information.'

A new window popped up with a ding sound and a woman in her mid-thirties showed her police badge. Nitesh's heart raced. She was in plain clothes.

'Nitesh Mishra, I'm DCP Madhavi Surve, Mumbai police crime branch.' Her voice was sharp, authoritative. 'You can verify my credentials on your screen.'

Nitesh squinted at the screen. The badge she showed looked official, but the words blurred together. His mind was unable to make meaning out of whatever his eyes were glossing over.

Sunlight filtered through the window grills, casting a prison cell like pattern on the wall around Nitesh.

'Are you paying attention, Nitesh?' Madhavi's voice cut through his thoughts.

'Y-yes, ma'am,' he managed to reply.

'Good. Because the situation has escalated.' She paused, letting the weight of her words sink in. 'Your details were found during a raid in a case involving the creation and distribution of pornographic material.'

Nitesh's world spun. 'No! That's impossible! I have nothing to do with . . .'

'Stop!' Madhavi Surve's command echoed through the speakers. 'Are you claiming you don't know Shilpa Shetty's husband Raj Kundra?'

'I-I only know of him . . . from the news,' Nitesh stuttered.

'What about Naresh Goyal?'

'The . . . the Jet Airways founder?'

'So, you do know him. Interesting. Your name has surfaced in a money laundering case connected to him as well.' Surve's voice dripped with suspicion.

'Please, you must believe me! I don't know these people personally! I am . . . I was a journalist, so I know about them.' Nitesh pleaded, his voice cracking.

'We'll see about that. For now, we are putting you under digital arrest. You will not leave the camera's view or disconnect this call without our permission.' Surve's tone left no room for argument. 'We're sending you a list of 452 questions. Answer them carefully—we already know the truth. Your responses will determine your level of cooperation.'

Nitesh felt the room closing in on him. His vision blurred and he slumped back in his chair, gasping for air.

'Mr Mishra!' Desai's voice snapped him back to reality. 'I understand this is overwhelming, but you have limited time. The questioning resumes in an hour. We will switch off our cameras now, but you need to be visible at all times. We are watching you.'

'I . . . I need to use the bathroom,' Nitesh whispered, his mouth dry.

'From now on, you need written permission for everything,' Surve interjected. 'Submit a formal request via WhatsApp to Officer Desai or email me directly. The clock is ticking, Mr Mishra. I suggest you focus on those questions.'

The faces in the chat windows were replaced by logos. Nitesh stared at his screen, reading through the multiple emails he had received from 'Mumbai Police'.

A faint rustle made him look towards the door. His wife Madhu stood nervously with a plate of food in her hand. Nitesh gestured her to stay out.

4

Tulika hurried through the gates of the faculty of arts. Normally she enjoyed the ten-minute leisurely walk from the GTB Nagar metro station but today she had rushed and was panting as a result. Tulika was very particular about sticking to her study schedule. She was late today because of Atul's send-off. The grandeur of the red brick building, a stark contrast to the cramped chaos of Mandawali, always filled her with a sense of purpose.

She looked for her study partners inside the library's cool and silent hall. They weren't there. Darting back outside, she spotted them—Priyal and Amit—at the tea stall nestled under the sprawling banyan tree. They seemed to be having a serious discussion. *They should have waited for me.* She assumed the conversation was about their studies. Tulika's eyebrows knitted together as she marched towards them.

'. . . you have to tell her, Amit. Dragging it out won't make it any easier,' Priyal said, her voice low yet insistent.

Amit sighed, running a hand through his hair. 'And what if she doesn't feel the same? What if she rejects me outright? Then I risk losing her friendship too.'

'But—' Priyal started, only to be cut off as Tulika stepped into their line of sight.

'Hello, you two!' Tulika's voice was a mix of curiosity and mild annoyance. 'Isn't this too early for a break? We have a schedule to keep.'

Amit straightened up, his expression shifting into a casual smile. 'Oh, hi Tulika. Just enjoying the weather. Perfect time for a tea break, isn't it?'

Tulika raised an eyebrow, nodding towards the pack of cigarettes peeking out of Amit's pocket. 'Or perfect *sutta* break for you?'

Amit chuckled, shrugging. 'Guilty as charged. But what to do, it's the ideal weather for an extra chai-sutta.'

Priyal rolled her eyes, giving Amit a subtle nudge. 'Yeah, yeah. We were just about to head in. We were wondering if you would make it today.'

'Atul's send-off took longer than expected.' Tulika glanced at her watch, anxiety creeping into her voice. 'I can't afford to fall behind schedule. The exam's only two months away and I've got so much ground to cover.'

Amit downed the last of his tea, crushing the paper cup in his hand. 'Right, let's go. Can't have future IAS officers slacking off.'

They started towards the library, Tulika leading the way. Priyal hung back slightly, whispering to Amit, 'The longer you wait, the harder it'll get.'

5

Radhika stretched her legs and arms while sitting in the chair. She had been making calls for hours, her voice growing hoarse from the effort. The clock ticked past 5 p.m.—another thirty minutes and one more ordinary day would have ended unremarkably. She called the next number that was in the excel sheet on her computer.

'Good evening, sir. This is Radhika Anand from Dream Home Developers. I am calling regarding our latest residential project?' she began, mustering as much enthusiasm as she could.

'Hello Radhika! How old are you?' The man's tone made her skin crawl.

She swallowed hard, her throat tight. 'I'm not allowed to talk about myself, sir. I have called to tell you about the features of our new launch.'

'I want to know about your features,' he chuckled. 'With that kind of voice, I'm sure you are a new property. Tell me about your hot features.'

Radhika's stomach churned as he continued, each word viler than the last. She glanced at her lead generation numbers for the day. They were woefully short. The pressure to meet the target weighed heavily on her.

'How old are you?' he repeated, more insistent this time.

Radhika hesitated, her desperation battling with her dignity. 'I'm twenty-eight, sir. Can I schedule a sales call . . .'

'Will you send me your picture?'

'I can't do that, sir,' she replied, her voice strained.

'How much do you earn . . . thirty thousand, thirty-five? I'll give you in one day what you earn in a month.'

The last shred of Radhika's patience snapped. '*BHENCHO!*' She slammed the phone down.

Radhika's hands shook as she tried to regain her composure. Vikram, a particularly annoying colleague who used the terminal to her right, leaned over her cubicle wall, a smug grin plastered on his face.

'Trouble with another call, Radhika? You know, if you just flirted a little . . .'

'Shut up, Vikram.'

'I'm just trying to give you some useful advice.' Vikram continued to grin.

'I don't need advice from a *chutiya* like you.' Radhika snarled, her eyes flashing.

Vikram's eyes widened. 'Arrey . . . easy there. I'm just trying to help . . .'

He should have kept quiet.

'Listen, dickhead . . .' The office fell silent, all eyes turning to Radhika. She didn't care. The dam had broken and a torrent of frustration poured out.

'*Munh band rakhaa kar kutte ki aulad, aglee baar khola toh advice ke saath poora guldasta gaand mei daal doongi.*' She pointed to the vase on the desk and made a shoving gesture that showed exactly what she meant.

Vikram retreated, his face red. Radhika turned back to her computer, a wicked gleam in her eye. 'I know what to do with such creeps.' She pulled up the caller's number from her call log and got to work.

First, she created a profile on an escort service website using his number and a stolen image of a model. Then, she systematically signed him up for every spam list she could find—erectile dysfunction treatments, weight loss miracles, hair loss, pet giveaways and even dating advice.

As a final touch, she posted his number on multiple online forums, advertising free relationship advice from a 'certified love guru'.

Satisfied with her handiwork, Radhika gathered her things and headed for the exit. She paused by Vikram's desk, leaning in close.

'Here's some real advice, chutiye. *Apni gaand mein ungli karke naak mein daal.* You'll smell your own bullshit.'

With that, she strode out, leaving a stunned silence in her wake.

Two

1

Atul stepped out of the arrival gate at Bangkok's Suvarnabhumi Airport, his eyes scanning the sea of faces for someone holding a sign with his name.

There, amidst the crowd, he spotted it—a white placard with four names neatly printed in black: 'Atul Anand, Maya Sahdev, Sudhakar Menon, Vikas Kumar.' A man in a crisp white shirt and dark trousers held it aloft, his eyes darting between the arrivals.

Atul approached him, his heart racing with excitement and a tinge of nervousness. 'Hello, I'm Atul Anand,' he said, extending his hand.

The man's face lit up with a practiced smile. 'Ah, Atul! Welcome to Bangkok. I'm Rajesh Iyer, HR, overseas lead for A-cent Tech Solutions.' He shook Atul's hand firmly. 'Let's wait for the others.'

One by one, the others joined them. Rajesh introduced them to each other. Maya, who looked like the youngest of them, seemed diffident, her fingers fidgeting with the strap of her shoulder bag. Sudhakar looked bewildered with the bustle of the airport around him while Vikas kept moving in excitement as he peppered Rajesh with questions about the workplace.

As they gathered their luggage, Rajesh cleared his throat. 'Now, there's been a slight adjustment to the plan,' he continued, speaking fast. 'We need you to start with some preliminary training at our specialized facility in Cambodia. It's only for a month and you'll be paid the normal salary.'

Atul was surprised. Cambodia? That wasn't part of the plan. He looked at the others. Sudhakar's face mirrored his concern, Vikas didn't seem to care and Maya glanced from one to the other.

'But . . . my visa is for Thailand,' Sudhakar said with a frown.

Rajesh waved his hand dismissively. 'Don't worry about that. We've got it all covered. Your e-visa has been applied for. It's a great opportunity, really. You'll get specialized training that'll put you ahead of the curve.'

Atul felt a nervous knot in his stomach. This wasn't what he had been told. He pulled out his phone, fingers trembling slightly as he dialled the number of Sharma ji, the agent in Delhi who had coordinated the interviews.

'Haan, Atul beta?' Sharma ji's familiar voice crackled through the speaker.

'Sharma ji, I am at the Bangkok airport. One HR person is here, but he says I need to go to Cambodia for training. Is this . . . is this normal?'

There was a pause on the other end, just long enough to make Atul uneasy. Then Sharma's voice came back, overly cheerful. 'Arrey, don't worry, beta! These big companies, they have their ways. If they're sending you for special training, it must be good, no? Just go with it. It's all okay.'

Atul thanked him and disconnected. He saw Maya whispering into her phone and called his father. Rajesh checked his watch impatiently. 'We need to move, the flight leaves in two hours.'

With a deep breath, Atul ended the call and put the phone back in his pocket.

Rajesh clapped his hands together. 'Alright, everyone ready? Let's go catch that flight to Phnom Penh!'

Atul shouldered his backpack and laptop bag and rolled his new suitcase as the group moved towards the departure gate. He had dreamed of this moment for so long—his first step into a new life, a chance to make his family proud. Now, as he followed Rajesh towards the departure gates, he had that uneasy feeling that some people get with a sudden change in plans.

2

Nitesh Mishra seemed to have somehow shrunk over the course of the day as he sat hunched over his laptop, his eyes bloodshot and his nerves frayed. The room that had once felt like his safe space, where he had written news reports and helped his two kids with their homework, now felt like a prison cell. Nine hours had passed since he had answered the call, each hour feeling like an eternity of fear and uncertainty.

A new voice crackled through the laptop, deep and authoritative. 'This is Officer Makhija from enforcement directorate—the ED. I'll be overseeing the final stages of this investigation.'

Nitesh's heart sank. Another official, that too from the feared ED. He rubbed his temples, trying to ward off the headache that had been building all day.

'Yes, sir,' he managed, his voice hoarse from hours of talking.

Outside the room, Nitesh's wife, Madhu, paced nervously. She had followed his instructions to the letter, keeping the children away and maintaining silence about the situation. Twice she had almost called her brother, a bank manager in Pune, but Nitesh's warnings about 'strict confidentiality' had stopped her.

Back in the room, Nitesh's screen was a maze of open windows—bank statements, investment portfolios and a seemingly endless questionnaire. He had answered over four hundred questions, each one more intrusive than the last. His eyes drifted to the family photo on his desk.

'Nitesh, we need you to consolidate all your funds into one account,' Makhija instructed. 'Have you completed the transfers into your one account as directed?'

Nitesh nodded, before speaking. 'Yes, sir. I've cashed out the FDs and moved everything to my savings account.' He paused, 'The PPF account I can't touch.'

'We know! Makhija replied, almost too quickly. 'We're trying to help you here, Nitesh. Don't let your non-cooperation force us to take more . . . severe measures.'

'And the mutual funds?' the voice of Vaibhav Desai chimed in.

'I've placed redemption requests for all of them.' The words felt like ashes in his mouth. All his life's savings.

Officer Makhija made a non-committal sound. 'Good. Now, as we explained earlier, all your accounts need to be temporarily frozen. So you need to transfer all the money to an RBI-controlled account for safekeeping during the investigation. I believe you have been given that account's details.'

'I . . . I've added the account to my savings account,' Nitesh said, his voice trembling. 'I will be able to transfer after twenty-four hours, transfers over fifty thousand takes that much time.'

'Yes, I know,' Makhija replied. 'This is standard procedure to prevent fraud.'

Madhu knocked softly on the door, her voice barely above a whisper. 'Nitesh? The children are asking about dinner.'

'Nitesh! We're losing valuable time here. Remember, your cooperation now will determine how lenient the courts will be.' Madhavi Surve's sharp rebuke left Nitesh no choice.

'Tell them I'm still working,' he called out to Madhu. 'I'll . . . I'll be out soon.' The lie tasted bitter on his tongue.

'Mr Mishra, we're nearing the end of this process,' Officer Makhija continued, his tone softening now. 'Once the funds are secured, we can move forward with clearing your name. You've been very cooperative and that will be noted in our report.'

Nitesh nodded mechanically, too drained to feel any relief. The 'digital arrest' had taken its toll, leaving him exhausted and disoriented. He glanced at the clock—nearly ten hours had passed since this ordeal began. Outside, the sun had set on Delhi.

3

The evening chaos of Mandawali seeped through the bathroom walls. The cramped ground floor builder flat seemed to absorb all the noise from outside—vendors' shouts, people speaking loudly, the honking of vehicles and a song blaring at high volume. Aseem leaned closer to the mirror, adjusting his fresh shirt. A grin appeared as he thought about Soni. He stepped out moving his lips in sync with the song—'Pehli Baar Mile'.

The rhythmic thud-thud-thud of a knife hitting a cutting board echoed from the kitchen. Radhika's frustration was finding its release in the vegetables before her.

'I can't take it anymore, ma.' Her voice trembled, whether from anger or hurt, it wasn't clear. 'Those creeps at work, the things they say on calls . . .' The knife came down with more force. 'I'm done.'

Tulsi wiped sweat from her forehead with her sari's pallu, steam rising from the dal she stirred. 'Keep your head down and do your work. Leave everything else to God.'

The familiar squeak of the front door announced Anand's return. He moved with the weariness of a man who had spent twelve hours navigating Delhi's merciless streets. Following his daily ritual, he went to their bedroom, which was almost directly opposite the kitchen, placed the auto keys on the pooja shelf and folded his hands before the gods.

Radhika stormed in with a glass of water. 'Papa, I can't continue my job.' The words erupted like water breaching a dam. 'Better to marry and run my own house than endure these . . . these . . .' She choked back the cuss words. 'I don't care whether the groom is fair or dark, good looking or ugly, as long as he has a permanent job.'

'Radhika!' Tulsi's ladle clattered against the pot. 'Careful how you speak in front of your father.' This was one of those rare occasions when Tulsi raised her voice.

Aseem caught Radhika's last outburst and thought it would ruin any little chance he had of getting money. He joined in, 'Quitting now would be selfish and stupid. You have a job, stick with it.'

'Oh, look who's talking about being selfish,' Radhika shot back, her eyes flashing. 'The most self-centred person on earth who can never see beyond his own toes.'

Aseem held up his hands, trying to placate his sister. 'Listen, just hang in there. A steady income will help you catch a better groom. And, once I have my gym running, I'll arrange a bigger, better wedding for you. Promise.'

'You mean once you have blown whatever money Atul sends on one of your stupid half-brained plans,' Radhika said with a smirk sharper than the knife she had used moments ago.

In the small bedroom she shared with Radhika, Tulika hunched further over her book, her pencil pressing harder into the paper. The constant background noise was bad enough without family drama adding to it.

Anand set down his water glass with deliberate care. 'Radhika, decisions made in anger rarely bring happiness.' He wiped his hands on a towel. His hands moved deliberately, matching the words as they came out of his mouth. 'I will find a suitable match within our means.' His eyes shifted to his younger son. 'And Aseem, if you want to start a business, first earn the investment yourself.'

Aseem's jaw clenched. 'But papa, this opportunity won't last . . .'

'Plans are good,' Anand's quiet voice somehow cut through the noise, 'but execution matters more.' He paused, adding almost as an afterthought, 'Atul had called. I missed it and now his phone is not reachable.'

No one felt this was abnormal. Aseem grabbed his helmet from the rusted hook by the door and bounded out. 'Going to meet a friend, will come back late.' Soni's house near Kingsway Camp was a good distance away and he didn't want to be late.

As he kick-started his bike, a different energy thrummed through him. He began humming the love song again. Tonight was about Soni, about exciting possibilities. The family drama could wait.

4

In the girls' bedroom, two single beds were set against opposite walls. A sewing machine, which also doubled as

Tulika's study table, stood between the two beds against the wall on the opposite side of the door. Tulika sat cross-legged on her bed with a Class 10 NCERT book in her lap. Going through Class 8 to 10 subject books from NCERT alongside a popular general studies guide was part of her study plan for UPSC's preliminary test. She looked up from her book and watched Radhika aggressively brush her hair. It had been going on for some time, as if she was trying to brush away the day's frustrations.

'Didi, are you fine?' she asked.

'Actually, I'm feeling a lot better now,' Radhika replied as she stopped brushing and started pulling hair from the comb.

'Tell me exactly what happened,' Tulika said softly.

Radhika's face broke into an unexpected grin. 'Oh, you should have seen that chutiya Vikram's face when I told him where he could shove his advice.' She mimicked his shocked expression, making Tulika giggle despite her concern.

'Was that the creep on the call?'

'No, that's my nosy colleague who thinks he's God's gift to humanity. The creep is going to be very busy answering calls about everything from erectile dysfunction to hair loss treatments.' Radhika's eyes gleamed with mischief. 'I signed him up for every spam list I could find. And created three dating profiles. He's now a forty-five-year-old divorced man desperately seeking love.'

Tulika tried to maintain a disapproving face but failed. Laughing, she said, 'Di, you're terrible!'

'He started it.' Radhika sat beside Tulika. 'Remember this, chhoti, being nice doesn't work most of the time. And it certainly never does with bad people. You keep being nice and people will walk all over you.'

Tulika had got the default nickname for the youngest daughter of most families in North India. She stopped smiling. 'But about quitting . . .'

'Don't worry so much, chhoti.' Radhika softened her tone. 'Which reminds me . . .' She moved closer on the bed. 'You need to stop killing yourself over this exam.'

'I'm not killing myself. Though I do feel that I have to clear it this time. Papa's hopes—'

'Are his hopes, not your life.' Radhika's voice turned serious. 'You're intelligent chhoti. And you have more discipline than me. I'm not saying stop studying hard, just don't be under pressure about it all the time. You used to love movies and songs, and now I don't see you ever listening to one or watching a movie.'

'There's so much left to study. When am I going to watch a movie?' Tulika sounded a little frustrated.

'Now! We're going to watch it now.' Radhika opened a streaming app on her phone. She inserted her earphones into the phone and extended one ear plug toward Tulika keeping the other one for herself. 'We'll watch a movie in instalments, twenty minutes each day,' Radhika said with a grin.

Tulika took the earplug but still looked unsure.

'You'll clear the exam this time. But you have to find breaks for relaxing too. And remember that getting into the civil service is your dream; you are not doing it for anyone else but you.'

'When did you get so wise, di?' Tulika teased with a mock concerned look and placed her hand on Radhika's forehead.

'Probably around the same time I learned to tell people where to shove their fake advice.'

The sisters giggled and then fell into comfortable silence. They started watching the movie on Radhika's phone. The shared earphones bridged their different worlds with the familiar comfort of sisterhood, much like the way their mother's dupatta had once linked their childhood games of 'train-train'.

Three

1

ASEEM'S HEART RACED AS HE WALKED down the narrow lane to Soni's house. He had parked his bike at a distance to avoid any attention. The cool night air gave him goosebumps, or maybe that was just his excitement.

He couldn't help grinning as he remembered meeting Soni at his friend's wedding last year. She was something else—laughing at his lame jokes, firing back with her own zingers. Classic Delhi girl, all sass and style. From day one, he was hooked.

Since then, it had been a rollercoaster of secret meetups and stolen moments. Mostly in dark movie theatres, where they would hold hands, sneak kisses and dream of more. But with the constant presence of family members in their respective homes, that's as far as they had gotten.

Aseem had been itching to ask Soni for a weekend getaway. Maybe Nainital or Mussoorie. Just the two of them—no parents, no siblings, no interruptions. But before he could work up the nerve, Soni one-upped him with tonight's invitation.

He was familiar with the area. He came to drop Soni often, but only up to the main road, a couple of hundred metres away. Never to the house. He would drive by it alone afterwards. Her family ran a general store on the ground floor and lived on the first. Today, as he climbed the stairs for the first time, his mind went into overdrive. All those times they had to cut short a kiss, all the hugs that lingered a bit too long but still felt a bit less, all the longing looks across café tables—was tonight the night when *it* was going to happen?

His heart pounded like he had just run a marathon. That cheesy love song was stuck in his head. He felt like the hero in his own romance movie.

Standing at her door, Aseem took a deep breath. His palms were sweaty and his mouth felt dry. His heart was now beating in sync with the rhythm of the song that played in a loop in his head—*Khanki payal masti mein* . . .

He ran his fingers through his hair and rang the bell. The door swung open, and there she was, her eyes wide, her mouth open, about to say something. But Aseem was too wired, too ready for this moment. He scooped her up in his arms and continued singing, '. . . *Do kangan khanke re*.' He turned around with her in his arms.

'Aseem, stop!' Soni hissed, her voice laced with urgency, 'Idiot . . . stupid . . .'

But it was already too late. '*Hamma hamma . . . hamma!*' He turned around and completed the song with a couple of pelvic thrusts—actually he meant to do two pelvic thrusts but had to stop at one and a half because they were sitting and staring at him. Her father, bristling with anger, her mother, her dupatta halfway to her mouth in surprise, and her younger brother Monu, his eyes wide in excitement.

Aseem froze, his voice trailing off mid-song. He slowly lowered Soni to the ground, his arms still around her, his eyes darting from one family member to the other. Soni wriggled out of his grasp, her face flushed with embarrassment.

'Papa, this is Aseem,' she said, her voice barely above a whisper. 'He's a . . . friend.'

Soni's father stood up, his eyes boring into them. 'Friend?' he growled. 'Do friends pick you like a sack of grain, singing . . . stupid songs!'

Aseem swallowed hard, trying to find his voice. 'Uncle, I . . . I'm sorry. I thought . . .'

'You thought what?' Soni's father interrupted, his voice rising. 'That you could come into my house and . . . and . . . what?' He spluttered, his face turning red.

Aseem's mind raced, trying to piece together what had gone wrong. He had been so caught up in the excitement of the evening, the prospect of finally being alone with Soni, that he hadn't even checked his phone since leaving the gym.

Soni, her face burning with embarrassment, stepped forward. 'Papa, I can explain. This is all a misunderstanding.'

She turned to Aseem, her voice low and hissing. 'I tried to call you. Left a message too. Didn't you see it?'

Aseem fumbled for his phone, his hands shaking slightly. As he pulled it out, he saw the missed call and unread message from Soni. His heart sank. There it was, straight and clear: 'Don't come. Parents home. Sorry.'

'I . . . I didn't check . . .' Aseem stammered, looking from Soni to her parents. 'I was on my bike, and I was so excited . . . I mean, I was in a hurry to . . .'

Monu, who had been watching the scene unfold with growing interest, piped up. 'Ooh, what were you two planning to do?'

'Monu!' Soni and her mother screamed in unison.

'Go to your room!' Soni blurted, her voice an octave too high.

Soni's father was on a roll. 'What kind of boy are you? Barging into my home . . . manhandling my daughter!'

'Papa, please,' Soni pleaded. 'Aseem is good. He's just . . . enthusiastic.'

Her father's face turned an alarming shade of purple. 'I've seen his type before. Smooth-talking roadside Romeos!'

Soni tried to interject, 'Papa, please listen—'

But her father silenced her with a sharp look. He turned back to Aseem, his eyes blazing. 'Here's what's going to happen, young man. You're going to walk out that door right now and you're never going to contact my daughter again. Do you understand?'

Aseem nodded, his throat dry. But Soni's father wasn't finished.

'And if I ever see you near my daughter or my house again,' he continued, his voice rising, 'I'll make sure you regret it. I have connections and I will make your life very difficult. Am I making myself clear?'

The room fell silent. Even Monu, who had been enjoying the drama, sensed the gravity of the situation and shrank back into his chair. Soni's mother stood with her hand over her mouth, her eyes darting between her husband and Aseem.

Aseem looked at Soni, who stood with tears glistening in her eyes. He wanted to reach out to her.

'I asked you a question,' Soni's father barked. 'Am I making myself clear?'

Aseem swallowed hard and nodded. 'Yes, uncle . . . yes, sir,' he said, his mind in overdrive, searching for the right things to say. 'I understand . . . I understand your . . . concern,' he looked at Soni and then finding a sudden burst of courage—or insanity—blurted out, 'I love Soni. I want to marry her.' The words tumbled out even as he saw Soni's eyes widen in shock, her mother gasp and her father's face turn an even darker shade of red.

'Marry! You think marriage is easy?' her father roared. 'What exactly do you do . . . other than sneaking into other people's houses?'

'I am a fitness trainer, sir.'

'And what do you have to offer? A lifetime supply of protein shakes?'

Aseem stood his ground. 'I have plans, sir. I'm going to start my own business.'

Soni's father scoffed. 'Plans? Everybody has plans!'

Aseem flinched, the words hitting too close to home. But he didn't back down. 'I made a mistake, uncle. But my intentions are not bad. I want to marry your daughter. I love her.'

Soni's father looked at him for a long moment, his expression unreadable. Then he sighed, 'Listen, Romeo. You may have good intentions, but Soni is my only daughter and I want the best for her. Right now, you're not it.'

Aseem felt a lump form in his throat. He looked at Soni, her eyes filled with tears, her lips trembling. He looked back at her father, his resolve strengthening. 'I promise you—I will be the best. I will be the man Soni deserves.'

Soni's father nodded, his expression softening slightly. 'I hope so. But until then, stay away. Either become worthy of marrying her, or forget about her. That's your only warning.'

Aseem nodded. He looked at Soni one more time with a look that said everything will be fine, before turning and walking out.

As Aseem left, he felt a mix of emotions—embarrassment, determination and a hint of hope. He had messed up royally, but in doing so, he had discovered that he didn't want to lose Soni.

2

Nitesh Mishra lay sprawled on the bed, his body exhausted but his mind refusing to shut down. The laptop on the table, its screen dark, seemed to mock him with its presence. It was turned towards him and the camera light was on.

He tossed and turned, replaying the events of the day in his head. The interrogation, the threats, the money transfers—it all swirled in a nauseating mix of fear and regret.

The kids were sleeping in his room tonight with Madhu. He could only imagine what she must be going through.

Nitesh's phone buzzed on the nightstand, making him jump. He reached for it, his heart racing, only to see it was a message from one of his old colleagues at the news agency. 'Hi Nitesh, heard you were looking for work. Got any leads?' Nitesh stared at the screen, a bitter laugh escaping his lips. If only they knew.

3

Anand, too, found himself unable to sleep. He kept staring at the ceiling as the day's events kept repeating themselves in his mind. It had been quite eventful, from Atul's bittersweet farewell to Radhika's outburst. Tulsi lay next to him, her face turned away. From her breathing, Anand knew she hadn't slept yet.

Atul had gone so far away to a foreign land, but for a good opportunity. Radhika needed to calm down; her frustration was understandable, but it pained him to see her so angry. He had failed to find a good match for her so far, but now with Atul sending money, that should change. The thoughts filled Anand with both hope and anxiety.

Tulika was focused—he just needed to make sure that she was not disturbed. She reminded him of his own unfulfilled dreams and he was determined to see her succeed where he couldn't. Aseem was a problem. He simply didn't want to work hard, always making big plans but looking for shortcuts. Anand sighed inwardly, wondering where he had gone wrong with his youngest.

He couldn't let Atul's money go to Aseem's schemes. Radhika's marriage was the priority. Only after that . . . but even then, could he trust Aseem to be responsible with money? The questions kept him awake.

An auto rumbled past their small house, a familiar song from an old Hindi film drifting through the window. For a moment, Anand felt a pang of nostalgia, remembering how he used to love listening to music and then sing along. He used to remember all of Kishore Kumar's hits.

'Have you heard from Atul again?' Tulsi's voice interrupted his thoughts.

'No,' Anand replied softly.

She turned to face him, 'Do you remember how scared I was when we left our village? Delhi made us stronger.' She placed her hand on Anand's chest.

'He will be fine too. You sleep now.'

4

Aseem's mind raced as he sped through the dimly lit streets, the cool night air doing little to calm him. He had declared his intention to marry Soni, but her father's scepticism was justified. Aseem knew he lacked the means to support a wife. Was he being brave, loyal or foolish? His only hope, the gym partnership, was proving out of reach. The only way he could make it happen was Atul's money. He knew his father wouldn't give him anything though—it was intended for Radhika's wedding. Aseem saw it differently. Investing in a gym would yield returns and it was better than spending it on a one-day wasteful celebration. The logic seemed irrefutable to him. Why could his family not see it like that? He had to make it happen, anyhow.

5

The vehicle carrying Atul, Sudhakar, Maya and Vikas approached an imposing gate. The journey from the airport had taken nearly two hours and the unfamiliar urban Cambodian landscape had gradually given way to isolated rural roads and finally a dense jungle.

The headlights of their large car illuminated the formidable gate, revealing a fortress-like structure that seemed more suited to a military compound than a training facility for an IT company. The walls loomed impossibly high, the top edges adorned with coils of barbed wire that glinted ominously under the glare of powerful lights.

As the gate creaked open, Atul's heart began to race. The vehicle rolled forward, entering an enclosed world that somehow felt wrong, even if he didn't know the source of that feeling. Guards armed with batons and stun guns stood at attention, their faces stern and unwelcoming. The young men exchanged worried glances, their earlier excitement about the job opportunity now replaced by a growing sense of dread. Vikas, who couldn't stop talking in the early part of their travel, had become silent. Sudhakar and Maya nervously fidgeted, their eyes darting from the scene outside to people's faces inside the car.

The gates closed behind them with a resounding clang, sending a chill through Atul's body. The sound seemed to echo the finality of their situation. They were now cut off from the outside world. As they were ushered out of the vehicle by stern-faced men in uniforms, the reality of his situation began to sink in. He couldn't shake the feeling that he had walked into something sinister and there was no going back.

Four

1

THE OVERHEAD LIGHTS SEEMED TO HEIGHTEN the nervousness on the faces of the people gathered in the conference room. Atul's eyes moved across his fellow trainees. Some others were looking around too. The room was silent, punctuated only by the occasional cough or shuffling of feet. Everyone was weighed down by questions, it seemed.

Last night, through his anxious haze, Atul had noticed two buildings inside the high-walled compound—one appeared to be three storeys tall, though he couldn't be certain due to his mounting unease at seeing the armed guards and barbed wire. The other was a large, shed-like structure. Once inside the multi-storey building, their passports were collected without explanation. Then, they were escorted to the top floor where Maya was separated from the group and led to another section, while the men were taken to their dormitory.

Earlier that morning, a shrill alarm had jolted Atul and the others from a tired but disturbed sleep. They were told to get ready and report to the Aqua Room, their current location. It was on the second floor of the central building—a stark hall with blue walls, twenty-plus chairs facing a white board and an aquarium with no fish in it. At precisely 7.30 a.m., the doors had swung open and two people had entered, a slender Chinese individual and a hefty Caucasian man whose nationality Atul couldn't determine—perhaps British or American, he speculated.

And now, the first man who had introduced himself as Mr Chu, the manager, paced at the front of the room, his shoes making disquieting sounds against the polished granite floor. Behind him, the bulky man whom he had introduced as the security chief, Mr Kovac, stood silently and just watched them.

'You have seven days,' Chu snapped in a high-pitched, shrill voice while distributing yellow lanyards and thick manuals. 'Seven days to transform into expert workers. There is no room for mistakes.'

Maya, her voice trembling slightly, raised her hand. 'Sir, what about our salaries? Do we need to provide our account details, or . . .'

Chu's eyes narrowed to slits. 'New accounts will be opened for you. We handle all financial matters internally.'

Vikas, sitting in front of Atul, quipped a bit too loudly, 'Feels more like we're joining the Chinese army than an IT company.'

He might have expected laughter in response but barely had the words left his mouth when Kovac moved with startling speed. The crack of his palm against Vikas' cheek echoed through the room, leaving everyone stunned.

It sounded like a gunshot to Atul, who instinctively moved back in his chair.

'We don't entertain insubordination,' Chu said coldly. 'Let that be a lesson.'

They were all shocked by this sudden and unexpected violence. They had seen the signs, but till that point had not really thought of themselves as the targets for it.

They were next led on a tour of the work area which occupied most of that floor. The massive hall stretched before them with rows and rows of computer terminals arranged in neat lines. The windowless space was lit by harsh fluorescent lights, making it impossible to tell the time of day. Security cameras hung from the ceiling, their red lights blinking constantly. Atul caught fragments of conversations from the terminals.

'Our programme hacks into the lottery system . . . just log into our app . . .'

'Ma'am, I assure you, this investment is guaranteed . . .'

'Sir, the police are involved now. You need to act quickly . . .'

Atul's mind raced. This was no IT data centre or training facility. His mind supplied an alternative and the thought hit him like a punch to the gut.

'You will be paired up,' Chu announced. 'Watch and learn from our experienced workers.'

Atul found himself alongside Vikas, both assigned to shadow a dead-eyed man who introduced himself as Sundar. As they observed, the true nature of their 'work' started becoming clearer.

'Just transfer the funds, ma'am,' Sundar said into his headset. 'I assure you—this is a special account for our A-list clients only. Your money will be invested through our special algorithm and you will see very high returns within months.'

Atul's blood ran cold as the words hovering inside his head settled into an understanding. This was a highly organized scam.

As the day wore on, a new fear took root in Atul's mind. The high walls, the armed guards, the isolation, the taking of their passports—this wasn't a temporary training facility. This compound could very well be their permanent workplace. The promise of Bangkok seemed like a distant, cruel joke now.

'Vikas,' Atul whispered during a brief lull, 'I don't think we're going back to Bangkok. This . . . this is it.'

Vikas, still not recovered from Kovac's slap, nodded grimly. 'We're in deep shit, bro. Who the hell slaps in an IT training?'

Kovac materialized suddenly behind them. 'Less talk, more work,' he growled. The baton which Atul had earlier noticed in Kovac's side holster was in his hand now.

Atul turned back to the screen that had been given to him and Vikas for the training, his mind close to being overwhelmed with panic and desperation. *He had to find a way out, had to alert someone on the outside. But how?* His eyes darted around—multiple guards in the room, the security outside and the high wall. *He could call his father!* But his phone was useless without international calling and Wi-Fi was available only in the work area. They had been made to deposit their phones before entering. *But what could his poor father do even if he found out? And wouldn't it crush him?*

Suddenly there was a lot of shouting and cursing. Near the terminals along the far wall, security guards had someone surrounded. During their tour, Atul had seen two men and one woman crowding one terminal. He had noticed because one of the men wore a khaki police uniform shirt over normal trousers. Now, he could see a baton being used followed by an eerie static sound that he could not place immediately. He could not see the person being beaten but he could hear screaming.

At eight in the evening, after more than twelve hours, they were herded up the stairs to the top floor where their spartan living quarters were located. The reinforced windows in their rooms had three-inch metal rods to prevent any escape. Beyond those thick rods, they could see the compound's abnormally high wall topped with electrified barbed wire, a constant reminder of their imprisonment.

'What are we going to do?' Vikas whispered, his usual bravado completely shattered. Sudhakar joined them. 'I heard some people saying that this one person made a mistake and lost the person they had trapped. They beat him really badly.'

'That must have been what the screaming and shouting was about just now,' Vikas said.

'Did you see, the guards gave him electric shock! The guns they carry are for that.' Sudhakar looked like he was going to cry any moment.

Atul stared at the barred window, and the high wall beyond them. 'I don't know . . . what we can do.'

2

The clock had ticked relentlessly towards the end of the mandatory 24-hour wait for transfers above Rs 50,000 to newly added accounts. The screen in front of Nitesh displayed his bank account balance: Rs 22,00,000. That number represented years of hard work and careful saving. On the other end of the Zoom call, the scammers in Cambodia too waited with bated breath, their eyes fixed on their own screens, anticipating the imminent transfer.

Nitesh's hand hovered over the touchpad. He hesitated.

Desai's voice came through his headphones, encouraging him. 'We understand you are nervous, but everything is going to be okay.'

Nitesh tried to move his fingers but he couldn't feel anything. All sensation had vanished. *I am going to have a stroke*, he thought.

'We are not going to wait forever, Nitesh. We have other cases to handle too.' The man who had introduced himself as the ED officer shouted.

Then immediately came the woman's voice—soothing, intimate, 'You have done the hard part, Mr Mishra. Don't worry . . . this is the final step.'

Slowly, mechanically, Nitesh's finger moved. He clicked 'Confirm' on the transfer page.

The scammers at the compound in Cambodia silently high fived each other, then the one posing as ED officer Makhija cleared his throat and asked, 'So, where's the rest of the money?'

Nitesh blinked, taken aback by the question. 'Rest? What do you mean, sir?'

'The mutual fund money,' the scammer replied impatiently. 'You said you had put the redemption request yesterday, did you not?'

'Yes sir, I have made the request.'

'Where is it then?' The scammer unknowingly threw a lifeline to Nitesh.

Confusion momentarily overrode Nitesh's anxiety. 'Sir, that takes three days to redeem and only then the money comes into the investor's account.'

A beat of silence stretched between them, heavy with unspoken tension.

'Yes, yes,' the scammer back-pedalled hastily. 'I meant keep checking . . .'

Something clicked in Nitesh's mind. A seasoned ED officer wouldn't make such a basic mistake about mutual fund redemption timelines. The odd feeling that had been niggling at the back of his mind suddenly crystallized into a sharp suspicion.

He needed a moment to think, to reassess everything that had happened. 'Excuse me,' he said. 'My wife is at the door with tea. I'll be right back.'

He found Madhu in the kitchen, worry etched deep into her face. 'Call somebody . . . call my friend Rajiv . . .

or call your brother,' he whispered urgently. 'Tell them what's happening. Something's not right.'

When Nitesh returned to his laptop, 'Desai' spoke almost in a fatherly tone, 'We really appreciate your cooperation so far, Nitesh. Very few people handle this kind of scrutiny with your level of dignity.'

'But we will need to keep you under digital arrest till the mutual fund money comes into your account and you transfer it to us.' The woman playing 'DCP Madhuri Surve' said.

Nitesh's mind raced. He needed more time to understand what was really going on. 'I'm sorry,' he blurted out, 'but I really need to use the bathroom. I'll be right back.'

He hurried out of the room, ignoring the protests and threats from the other end of the call. He could have gone to his wife or made some calls himself. But he was so nervous he actually locked himself in the bathroom and waited there till Madhu knocked. He opened the door. Madhu looked anxious.

'Nitesh,' she whispered frantically, 'I spoke to my brother and with Rajiv too. They say it's a scam. Don't transfer any money.'

The words hit Nitesh like a physical blow. A scam. All of it—the interrogation, the threats—it had all been an elaborate, convincing, ruthless con. Nitesh had lost a major part of his savings, escaping total ruin more by luck than by his own doing. He stumbled back to his desk.

With a decisive click, Nitesh ended the call. Not satisfied with just that, he switched off the internet connection. He stood a while in confusion before slumping in his chair. The full weight of what had happened crashed down upon him. He should have seen through it. The improbability of the whole setup. He was a journalist, trained to question everything. But he hadn't.

What blinded him was fear. A deep, buried dread of the police, of government officials, of being caught in something he couldn't control. And they had preyed on that. Expertly.

The money was gone. But what would stay with him—what would gnaw at him for years—was the shame.

Madhu came and wrapped his head in her arms. They cried.

3

Atul's family sat quietly in their living room. Only Tulsi was in her bedroom after pacing back and forth for some time. Some drunk person was shouting outside but none of them reacted to that.

The two cotton mattresses that served as Atul's and Aseem's bed at night were still stacked in the corner. Anand sat in one of the two plastic chairs, trying to appear strong though inside he was no less worried than his wife. He wanted to reassure everyone, but his heart said it was so unlike Atul. It had been more than twenty-four hours since his missed call. Atul hadn't called again and his phone was still unreachable.

Radhika broke the silence. 'Maybe he's busy with work,' she suggested, her voice light but without conviction. 'Or the network is bad. Maybe he just forgot to charge his phone.'

Aseem fidgeted beside her. His mind was torn. On one hand, he was thinking about Atul; on the other, desperation for money gnawed at him. His gaze moved between his father and the floor, unwilling to meet anyone's eyes. 'Or what? Obviously, he would be busy with the training programme. It goes on the whole day. And he must have forgotten to activate international calling.'

'But he called from Bangkok,' Radhika said.

Tulika sat across from them, her phone in hand. She refreshed Atul's WhatsApp profile for the umpteenth time. Each time she hoped for that familiar 'last seen' status, yet it remained unchanged. No blue ticks. Nothing. She felt frustration swell within her. Why wouldn't he respond?

'That was a Wi-Fi call, must have been from the airport,' she reasoned.

Anand finally spoke up, breaking the uneasy silence. 'Does anyone know anything more about Atul's job?' he asked. 'Who did he speak with, any contact number?'

Radhika bit her lip, trying to recall anything useful. 'There was someone who set up the job,' she said. 'But all the details must be on Atul's laptop or his phone.'

Aseem, with his head lowered, added, 'He had received a link to apply for the job. But that's all I know. He didn't share any details and I didn't . . .' His voice trailed off, as if realizing he had been more concerned about himself than his brother.

Meanwhile, Tulsi lit a diya in front of her little shrine. She murmured prayers for Atul's safety. Whenever she didn't have an answer for something, she left it to her gods. It gave her strength.

Anand tried to comfort his family. 'It's only been a day, there could be any number of reasons. What do we know about a foreign job or how things work in foreign countries?' He looked at his wife and gave her a hopeful smile, 'Everything will be alright.'

'Our Atul is a good boy. Bhola Baba will protect him,' Tulsi added in a calm, determined voice.

Five

1

ATUL SAT HUDDLED IN A CORNER of the small, dark room, his knees drawn up to his empty stomach, trying to keep away the hunger. His throat burned with thirst. The small water bottle they had given him had been emptied hours ago. His stomach twisted painfully, a constant reminder that he hadn't eaten since breakfast yesterday. Now it must be around the afternoon, he guessed. They had said twenty-four hours, but he had no idea when he would be released. He needed to eat something.

Two days had passed since that fateful briefing. Two days since he was handed that damning manual. It had step-by-step instructions for scams. A training guide to fleece people. Not just one type, but a whole catalogue of deception.

The manual had details of how to lure victims into fake investment schemes. It was named Pig Butchering because the victims were slowly reeled in by gaining their confidence and showing them profits, before taking all their money. Then there was the Lottery Scam, a devious ploy involving two apps—one legitimate, one fake—designed to fleece hopeful gamblers. There was the Romance Scam, where older wealthy women were targeted, and the Sex Scam, where men listed on dating sites were enticed to pay for membership of non-existent clubs with the promise of sending them girls. A whole section on Digital Arrest scams, where the victim was told about a parcel from overseas that contained drugs, an Aadhaar card that had been misused, a phone number linked to illegal activity, or a family member caught committing a crime, then threatened and scared by people posing as government officials.

Atul wanted to run, to scream, to throw the manual across the room. But he did none of those things. Instead, he sat there, frozen, feeling utterly helpless.

The next day they were ordered to create fake profiles.

'Twenty profiles,' Chu had ordered in his sharp reedy voice. Ten as pretty women. Young and successful, the kind men dream about. Ten as attractive young men, who will be liked by rich older women. 'Create stories, make them all believable.'

Atul had hesitated. He didn't try to see what others around him were doing but he couldn't bring himself to start. It felt wrong, so fundamentally wrong.

The manager's voice cut through Atul's thoughts. 'You've got quotas to meet. Two hundred connections a day. That's why you need multiple profiles.'

Sudhakar, sitting next to Atul, leaned over and whispered, 'Just do it, man. It's not worth the trouble.'

But Atul couldn't. He stared at the blank screen, his mind reeling. How had he ended up here? This wasn't what his life was going to be. This was . . . criminal.

The manager was still addressing the room. 'You need to keep track of which profile you're using with each mark. Write it down, memorize it. These stories are your lifelines. Mess them up, and you're useless to us.'

Atul thought of his family back in Delhi. What would they think if they knew? His father, who had done hard honest work, driving an auto for decades. His devout simple mother, who had sacrificed so much for her children. He couldn't do this to them.

Minutes passed. Atul's screen remained blank. He couldn't bring himself to type a single word.

The manager noticed. His face twisted with anger. He held Atul's hair and shook him violently. 'Stop dreaming, you are here to work.'

'I can't do this,' Atul stammered.

'What can't you do? You think this is a joke?' he spat in anger, spraying saliva. 'You need to learn a lesson.'

Two guards yanked Atul up by the arms.

'Maybe some alone time and an empty stomach will clear your head,' the manager sneered.

That's how Atul had ended up in this tiny, dark room. No food, barely any water. The hours stretched endlessly.

His family would be worried sick by now. It had been three days since he had tried to call his father from Bangkok airport. He tried to stand, his legs weak and shaky. He could picture his mother pacing anxiously, muttering prayers under her breath. His father would be putting on a brave face, reassuring everyone even if he was the most worried person on the inside. A sob caught in Atul's throat. He had come here with such hope, such ambition. He was going to make his family proud, ease their financial burdens. Instead, he had got himself trapped in this nightmare.

The lock clicked and the door swung open.

A figure stood in the doorway, backlit and imposing. 'I trust your mind is clear and ready now.'

Atul's heart raced. He wanted to speak, to beg for release. But his parched throat produced only a weak croak.

'Your stubbornness is . . . inconvenient,' the manager said. 'But not unexpected. Many have sat where you sit now. All eventually see reason.'

Atul found his voice, though it came out as little more than a squeaky, hoarse whisper. 'Please . . . I can't do this. Let me go home.'

Manager Chu's laugh was sharp and humourless. 'Go home? Boy, you misunderstand your situation. You have a lot to learn and debts to clear.'

He snapped his fingers and a guard appeared in the doorway. 'Take him to the showers. Clean him up. Then bring him to my office. It's time we had a proper conversation about his future.'

2

As he sat on the worn-out two-seater sofa in their living room, Aseem didn't have a plan that could answer all the questions in front of him probably for the first time in his adult life. His family was in a state of helpless panic with no news of Atul. They had called the company's board numbers only to be told that there was no such recruitment. His father had gone to the police too. But he didn't have anything to prove that something wrong had happened.

On the other hand, Ravi, his potential partner had put him on a timeline; either Aseem came up with the money in three days, or he was going ahead with another partner.

Aseem's phone buzzed against the glass-top centre table. Soni's smiling photo lit up the screen. His thumb hovered over the answer button before he let it ring out. He knew what Soni wanted to know and that was another question he didn't have an answer for. The phone fell silent, only to buzz again with a text message:

Babu, call me! Have you talked to your family about us? A couple of heart and kiss emojis followed the message.

He clicked the phone screen off, but not before another message popped up:

BTW, still waiting for that proper proposal you promised. Make it special! This time it had a sparkling ring emoji.

The messages kept coming:

Papa is still angry about how you barged in that day.

But don't worry, I told him you have big plans. Just need to show him you're serious.

Aseem tossed the phone face-down beside him. The weight of his impulsive declaration at Soni's house pressed down on him. He had promised her father a stable future, promised Soni a dream proposal, promised Ravi the gym investment—all hanging on money that he didn't have, expecting it to come from Atul.

The creaking sound of the main gate announced his father's arrival. Tulsi came in from the kitchen, looking expectantly. Behind her, Radhika and Tulika also came into the small room. Everyone wanted to know if Anand had heard from Atul, knowing very well that the first thing he would have done in that case would have been to call home and tell them immediately.

Aseem vacated the sofa for his father and took the plastic chair. Anand just shook his head in negative while sitting. 'Went to the police station again. Same thing. They said he's an adult who went abroad willingly.' Anand sighed. 'Without proof of foul play, they can't do anything.'

Radhika snorted. 'Typical. When do the police ever help people like us?'

She could have gone on but for the call from her office. Radhika stared at the screen, her finger hovering over the decline button.

Anand looked at her as the call went unanswered.

Radhika shook her head. 'It's my office and I don't want to deal with them right now.'

Her phone started ringing again almost immediately.

Radhika made an exasperated sound, but she answered the call this time. 'Hello, yes?'

As she listened, her expression changed from annoyance to surprise. 'What? Why?' She waited for the answer from the caller and then said, 'Okay. I will come.'

She looked at her father, 'My boss, the owner of the company, wants to meet me. I will throw the resignation letter on his face before he fires me.'

Aseem, who had been silent until now, spoke up. 'Do not resign, apologize. We need the money, especially with no news from Atul.' Then looking at his father he blurted, 'Papa, I really need the money for the gym. I will ret—'

'I don't have money. Why don't you understand?' Anand replied even before Aseem could finish.

'The money you have kept for Radhika's marriage, I will return it soon.'

'And that is to be used for Radhika's marriage only.' Anand stood up and went inside. Radhika gave him a burning look and went after her father. Tulsi stayed there for a moment, her eyes threatening to overflow, then she returned to the kitchen.

Aseem sank back into the sofa his father had vacated moments earlier, gripping his head in an attempt to quell his frustration. Tulika, the last person remaining in the room, jabbed her younger brother's head with her finger, 'God must have forgotten to put something here when he made you. Asking for money at a time like this!' she chided, though her tone remained light.

Aseem looked up at his sister and put on a very serious expression. 'You know, you were born only because they wanted a second son—me. So, open your mouth in front of me only to say thanks, not to lecture!' By the time he finished speaking, a mischievous grin had spread across his face, the kind that had always irritated his sister since childhood.

'You keep talking nonsense like this and, one day, I'll seal your mouth while you're asleep!' Tulika shot back, her hands planted firmly on her hips, though the corners of her mouth twitched with the hint of a smile.

'Wait till I pour an entire bottle of glue in your hair!' Aseem threatened.

'You dare not! Juice Centre's John Abraham?' Tulika went for Aseem's most vulnerable point. He was not very proud that the only accomplishment of his modelling dreams was a picture on a juice cart's banner. 'I hope you are at least getting some free juice?' Tulika laughed.

'Listen Thulli–' Aseem improvised the not so flattering Delhi slang for a cop.

'Don't you dare call me that' Tulika's voice rose.

'Thulli. Perfect name for a wannabe police officer.' Aseem got up and started walking in a way that could have only been described as a limping penguin walking with a stick. 'You'll look funny in that khaki uniform, strutting around with a stick.'

'Don't call me that!' She picked up a cushion from the sofa and hurled it at him.

'Or what? You'll arrest me?' Aseem caught the cushion effortlessly. 'Charge me under Section Thulli-20?'

'I swear to God, Aseem–'

'Officer Thulli reporting for duty!' He stood up and gave an exaggerated salute.

'I am going to study. I have better things to do in life than talk about your moronic plans.' Tulika sulked.

Aseem caught her by the wrist as she tried moving past the centre table, not letting her go.

'Let me go. You're such a horrible person!' She screamed. 'Ma . . .'

'Aseem. Don't trouble her.' Their mother's voice from her bedroom cut through their fight.

'Go, cribber, go.' Aseem left her hand, 'Ma's crying baby . . . eee . . .'

A pillow that was stacked above the mattresses smacked in his face before he could complete what he was saying. He picked it up and threw it back at her but by then Tulika had run away to her room. He smiled.

3

The office was bare except for a desk with a computer, an oversized leather chair in which Chu looked even smaller and a printer on a small table in one corner. The air conditioner seemed set at a low temperature or perhaps it was the size and bareness of the room; either way, Atul could feel himself shivering because of the cold. He had been given time for a quick bath and a quicker meal before being dragged and shoved unceremoniously into this room. The guard still stood behind him.

'Now,' the manager began, sliding a sheet of paper across the desk, 'let's discuss your debt.'

Atul's eyes widened as he scanned the document. It was a list of expenses: payment to the agent, transportation costs, accommodation, food, even a charge for 'orientation'. The total at the bottom made his head spin.

'Twenty thousand dollars?' Atul gasped. 'This . . . this is impossible!'

The manager's lips curled into a humourless smile. 'You have two options. Work to pay off the debt or your family pays it off for you.'

'This is wrong!' he protested. 'I didn't agree to any of this. My family can't pay this much. They're depending on me to send money, not the other way around.'

Chu's expression didn't change. 'You were brought here to do a job. Remember, you have signed a contract. You work, you pay off your debt. Simple.'

'But this isn't fair! I was brought here under false pretences!' Atul cried out. 'You can't just kidnap people and force them to work for you!'

The manager sighed, exchanging a look with the guard. 'It seems our friend is still confused about his situation. Help him understand.'

The guard's fist connected with Atul's stomach, driving the air out of him. He doubled over, gasping for breath. Another blow made him fall to the floor and kicks followed. Chu waited till the guard stopped.

'Let me make this clear,' Chu said, his voice like ice. 'You have two choices. Work for us, or your family pays. If you do well, you'll not only earn money but also enjoy certain . . . perks. Girls, alcohol, drugs. Whatever you want.'

The guard pulled Atul back on his feet and held him straight.

Chu leaned back in his chair, his eyes narrowing. 'Be smart. Once you pay off your debt, maybe you'll go back home one day.'

Atul's heart sank. He was well and truly trapped.

'I . . . I'll work,' Atul whispered, defeat echoing in his voice. The guard removed his hand and he slumped forward slightly, his head bowed.

'Excellent,' Chu nodded, a cruel smile playing on his lips. 'Welcome aboard.'

4

Radhika entered the large, yet somewhat disorganised office of Dream Home Developers Pvt Ltd, expecting to meet the elderly owner, Radheshyam Gupta. Instead, she found a young man doing a headstand against a wall. His perfectly ironed shirt had come untucked, revealing a sliver of skin. The walls were adorned with photographs of previous and ongoing projects while piles of brochures rested in the corners of the room.

She stood there, unsure whether to wait or leave, when the man spoke, still upside down.

'Ah, you must be Radhika. Please, take a seat.' His voice was surprisingly steady for someone in that position.

Before Radhika could respond, he gracefully came down from the headstand, only to immediately stand on one leg, eyes closed, arms spread like a flamingo.

'I'm Jayesh,' he said, maintaining perfect balance. 'My father asked me to handle your . . . situation.'

Radhika's fingers brushed against the resignation letter in her open shoulder bag. So this was the owner's son. She had heard about him returning from abroad, but this was not what she had expected.

'Sir, about the incident—' she began.

'Please,' he switched legs with fluid grace, 'call me Jayesh. And yes, about that incident. Father wanted me to . . .' he wobbled slightly, opened his eyes and finally planted both feet on the ground. 'Actually, why don't you tell me your version first?'

'I don't regret what I did,' Radhika stated firmly, placing her resignation letter on his desk.

'You mean, creating fake profiles of a potential client?' Jayesh asked. 'And signing him up for . . . let's see . . .' he glanced at a paper on his desk, 'erectile dysfunction treatments.' he snorted, quickly covering the oncoming grin with a cough.

'He deserved worse,' Radhika's voice was steady. 'I'm not going to apologize for standing up to sexual harassment. Or about Vikram—'

'Ah yes, Vikram,' Jayesh interrupted. 'The one you suggested should . . . how did the HR complaint put it . . . "perform an unnatural act involving his own posterior, finger and . . . nose"?' He chuckled and his face turned red—though possibly from having been upside down. 'I had to look up half the Hindi words you used. Very educational.'

'The person could be getting hundreds of calls daily; he could file a case against us,' he continued.

'Let him try taking legal action,' Radhika lifted her chin. 'The call is recorded.'

'Oh, we heard it,' Jayesh grinned openly now. 'Father was furious, of course. Though you should have seen his face when he was reading the part of the complaint where you told Vikram about the . . . what was it . . . "guldasta"?'

He put on his suit jacket, attempting to look serious but failing miserably. 'As your boss, I should be appalled. But as someone who's been in countless mind-numbing client meetings since coming back, I'm taking notes.'

Jayesh picked up the letter, glanced at it and smiled—a charming, slightly nervous smile that didn't quite match his expensive suit and carefully styled hair. 'Would you believe me if I said I was impressed?'

'Impressed?' Radhika's eyebrows shot up in surprise.

'We're . . . I am having some . . . issues at one of our construction sites,' he said, and as if struck by a sudden thought, 'Actually, it is my first project and I am having problems dealing with it. I think some shady things are going on.'

'Shady?' Radhika asked, trying to process this unusual situation.

'Stealing . . . overcharging, I don't know. But I am sure someone is lining his pockets. I can use someone to sort it out. Someone with your . . . assertiveness.' He started to look nervous, 'Father wants me to handle this project to prove myself, you see. But I am not good with confrontation; I need someone who is.'

'You want *me* to handle it?'

'I want us to fix it together, Radhika.'

'But . . . I don't know anything about construction or management.'

'You've got the most important qualities needed. You're honest, you're brave and you don't put up with nonsense. The rest, we can learn together.'

'I . . . I don't know what to say,' she stammered.

'Say yes. If we can turn this project around, there will be a bigger role for you here.' He smiled and it reached his eyes. 'Also, I could really use someone who isn't freaked out by my . . . unusual coping mechanisms.'

Radhika's mind was reeling. When she walked into this office, she had expected to be fired and was ready to resign. Instead, she was being offered an opportunity by this strange, intriguing man who seemed to defy gravity when anxious.

'When do we start?' she heard herself say.

His face lit up. 'Right now. But first, would you mind if I did one more headstand? Just thinking of confrontation makes me nervous.'

For the first time that day, Radhika smiled.

5

'*Chai achhee hai.*' Radhika smiled as she took an appreciative sip, settling down on an overturned bucket near where the workers were having their afternoon tea break. They acknowledged her with wary nods. She had been trying to talk to them for the past hour, but had only received monosyllabic responses.

'You know,' Jayesh spoke up from where he stood, slightly apart, 'if we can't fix things and bring the project on track, it will be shut down.'

Some of the workers exchanged worried glances.

'Shut down?' an older worker asked.

'Hmm,' Radhika took a sip of her tea. 'Delays, over-budget, work stoppages. The signs are not good, the company is not left with many choices, but we can still save it. If you all help us understand what is wrong.'

One young worker muttered, 'Everything is wrong.'

'So, tell me why? Two floors should have been completed by now, but we are still at the parking levels. Why are we so behind?' Radhika pushed.

More exchanged glances.

'Work had to be stopped many times,' someone said.

'The company makes money but does not pay us overtime.'

'Yes. They make us sign for double the amount we are paid. So they don't have to pay taxes.'

'Careful what you say,' one worker warned.

'No, let him speak.' Jayesh stepped closer, his voice gentle. 'Please. We need to understand. Who makes you sign for double the amount you get?'

There was a moment of silence. Then someone from behind spoke. 'Same one who signs for 100 bags of cement and asks us to make do with seventy.'

Some people sniggered. Radhika and Jayesh looked at each other.

'I have a feeling who that is. But it will be easy to deal with if you give me the name,' Jayesh said.

Before anyone could answer, a shadow fell over them.

'What's going on here?' site supervisor Gautam's voice boomed. 'Why are the workers not at work?'

'Just having a small chai break, Gautam ji,' Radhika smiled pleasantly. 'Learning some interesting things about our site operations.'

'Office work shouldn't be done on site, madam. Too much dust.' He turned to Jayesh. 'Sir, you should go back to the office. I will answer any question you . . .'

'The questions are why we're here,' Radhika cut in. 'Like why the numbers don't match on purchase orders, the entry log at the godown and what finally comes to the workers. What are you doing with money that the company pays for workers if you are giving them only half of it?'

Gautam's face darkened. He didn't know that Radhika had gone through every purchase order, every delivery receipt, every payment record—in short, any paper she could lay her hands on in the three days since her first meeting with Jayesh.

'You should not be roaming around on the site, madam,' Gautam growled, 'It is not a safe place for women and accidents happen all the time.'

Radhika's eyes flashed as she stepped up to him and smiled, '*Ye toh wo baat ho gayee—ulta chor kotwal ko daante!* Look at the pot calling the kettle black. *Pant utarne wali hai Gautam. Fataafat kat le varnaa nanga daurta nazar aayega.*'

The workers guffawed and giggled. Some moved threateningly towards Gautam, but Radhika stopped them. Gautam's head had bowed down, his momentary bravado gone. Radhika turned to Jayesh, 'Should I call the police, or would you prefer to handle this internally?'

Jayesh, who was hanging on every word she said, straightened and found his voice. 'Father will decide what to do with him. Till then every order and every payment will go through you. Gautam, you will report to Radhika and you better behave. Any trouble you create and I will file a police case myself.'

After Gautam left, Jayesh and Radhika retreated to the site office. As soon as the door closed, Jayesh slumped against the wall.

'That was insane . . .' he started.

'Are you okay?' Radhika asked, genuine concern in her voice.

'I'm fine,' he managed a weak smile. 'Just . . . confrontations aren't my strong suit.'

'I can clearly see that. Well, that's why you have me,' Radhika said, then quickly added, 'For backup, I mean. Professional backup.'

'You are good. You are insanely good.' Jayesh said with a smile and then added. 'Thank you. For stepping in. For everything.'

Their eyes met, and for a moment, something unspoken passed between them. Then Radhika cleared her throat.

'We should start checking the other records. Who knows what else he was up to?'

'Right,' Jayesh straightened. 'Back to work.'

Six

1

THE COMPOUND'S OPPRESSIVE ATMOSPHERE had become Atul's new reality over the past two weeks. The young man who had left his home in Delhi with exciting dreams now went through his days with a defeated look in his eyes. From his workstation in the vast hall on the middle floor, he could see rows upon rows of others like him, working under the watchful eyes of the guards. The harsh glow of the lights made the whole scene feel even more surreal. He was like someone put in a prison without committing a crime and with no idea when the trial would start. The jungle beyond the walls added to Atul's feeling of hopelessness.

The constant whirring of surveillance cameras, combined with the occasional crackle of electricity from the barbed wire, created an eerie soundtrack to their captivity. Supply trucks would come through the heavily guarded main gate twice a week, their arrival marking the only break in the monotony of their confined existence. The guards with their stun guns would become extra vigilant during these deliveries.

Atul had quickly learned that resistance came at a steep price. His own initial reluctance had earned him beatings and starvation, but these punishments paled in comparison to what he had witnessed others endure. The sight of a fellow captive—the one whose error had inadvertently let Nitesh off the hook—remained etched in Atul's mind. The man's body was covered in bruises and one of his ears was horrifically absent. Atul had witnessed another desperate individual make a frantic escape attempt through the gates that had opened for the supply truck, only to be chased by the guards in an SUV and run over. He hadn't been seen again.

The few women among the captives presented an even darker side to this operation. Maya, the girl who came with him, occupied the workstation diagonally across from his. Her eyes carried a constant haunted look. Atul had seen her being taken away by the guards, returning hours later with a vacant stare. She would sit silently at her station, her trembling fingers betraying the horror she had endured. The other women's faces told similar stories—their punishment for resistance or poor performance went beyond beatings. Atul heard stories of sexual abuse and forced participation in pornographic videos. It made his stomach turn.

The static buzz of stun guns had become a familiar sound but it still sent shivers down his spine. He had seen the guards use them indiscriminately, sometimes purely for their own twisted amusement. The routine brutality of their captors had gradually worn down Atul's resolve.

He had created multiple fake profiles on Facebook as instructed. They were with male and female identities, using pictures from the internet, some of them of popular Indian models. He was supposed to contact 200 people every day with offers of lucrative investment opportunities. Once a person showed interest, he was to bring them into a WhatsApp group from where the more experienced people would take over. If the supervisors felt he was not trying hard enough to convert the contacts to potential victims, it invited punishment.

Though he had surrendered to his circumstances, a new determination had crept in. He had to connect with his family. Just to let them know that he was alive. He knew what his parents would be going through with no word from him for two weeks. Atul decided to reach out to Aseem. His younger brother, despite his flaws, had always been resourceful. More importantly, contacting Aseem would give him a way to spare his parents some details of the horrifying situation he was in.

Atul steeled his mind against fear and typed out a message even as his heart raced:

My job was a scam. I am somewhere in Cambodia. Don't know where but in a compound with high walls that has barbed wire on top. Not allowed to leave. Agent cheated me. R.K. Sharma, K-29A Kalkaji. Tell ma–papa I am ok. Tell me you have seen the message so I can delete it.

To Atul's relief, Aseem responded almost immediately. With many questions, like why hadn't Atul called for so long, what did he mean by 'not allowed to leave'. It was unthinkable for Aseem that his brother had become a slave—as the possibility would have been for Atul himself till two weeks ago.

Atul quickly provided some details of his captivity and the deception that had led him there. He asked Aseem to choose carefully what to tell their parents so as not to cause panic. Atul swiftly deleted the conversation and prayed afterwards that the exchange would go unnoticed by his captors.

But he had not had luck on his side lately. The next thing Atul knew, Kovac, the burly security chief, was looming over him, flanked by two stone-faced guards. Kovac's cold eyes bore into Atul as he growled in a low, menacing voice.

'What message did you send to your brother?' They either already knew his family details or it didn't take much to link Atul Anand and Aseem Anand.

Atul felt fear coursing through his veins. 'I . . . I made a mistake,' he stammered, his voice barely above a whisper. 'I just wanted to let my family know I was safe.'

Kovac's eyes narrowed dangerously. 'Why did you delete, if it was just that?'

Atul's heart pounded; breathing became more difficult each moment. 'I . . . I was scared. I panicked.' He desperately searched for more words to keep them from hurting him which was becoming a certainty with each passing moment.

The assault seemed to last an eternity. Kovac's fist connected with Atul's jaw, sending him sprawling from his chair. Fists and boots rained down as he curled into a protective ball, trying desperately to shield himself. After a while his mind went into a haze. And he stopped feeling pain.

Through the fog, Atul could hear Kovac barking orders at the guards. Rough hands seized him, dragging his limp body across the floor. Atul almost felt relieved when he was thrown into a small, windowless room. The darkness provided a comforting embrace and after some time, he drifted off to sleep or maybe it was unconsciousness.

2

Aseem didn't know what to do. He moved around the house filled with panic and confusion. He glanced at his mother, busy in the kitchen preparing dinner. *Will they be able to eat anything tonight?*

'Beta, why are you so restless?' Tulsi called out.

'Nothing, ma,' Aseem replied, his voice strained. He checked his phone again. 6.15 p.m. His father would come home only after 8. Radhika wouldn't be home until even later—her job kept her out longer these days. He thought of talking to Soni but then decided not to. He had told her Atul was the one funding his investment.

The metal grill main gate creaked, followed by the wooden door opening, and Tulika walked in. Aseem pulled her into the girls' room, closing the door behind him.

'What's wrong?' she asked, concern clouding her face. Aseem immediately gestured to keep her voice down.

'I need to tell you something,' he whispered.

As Aseem recounted Atul's message, Tulika's expression shifted from concern to shock to horror. She sank onto the bed, her hand covering her mouth, eyes wide with disbelief.

'*He Bhagwan*,' she choked on her words. 'This . . . can't be happening.'

Aseem nodded, running his hands through his hair. His panic now mirrored in his sister's face. 'I don't know what to do. Should I tell ma?'

Tulika shook her head, her mind reeling. 'No. I think we should wait for papa.'

They sat in tense silence, each lost in their own troubled thoughts. Aseem's leg bounced nervously while leaning against his mother's sewing machine, while Tulika twisted her dupatta between her fingers. The ticking of the clock on the wall had become very loud.

3

The sound of the front door jolted them both from their anxious, paralytic wait. They rushed to the living room, just about slowing down while crossing between the kitchen and their parents' room so as not to alarm their mother. Anand's tired face broke into a weak smile seeing them. However, his expression quickly changed as he saw the look on their faces.

'What's wrong?' Anand asked, his voice low. Almost instinctively feeling the need to not make his wife a part of it.

Aseem and Tulika exchanged a glance, silently debating how to proceed. They led their father to the girls' bedroom, hoping to have a conversation without involving their mother. But in their small house, there wasn't much one could hide. Tulsi heard the hushed tones. She appeared at the doorway, her eyes filled with concern. 'Why are you all whispering? What's happened?'

No one spoke for a moment, but not saying anything wasn't an option anymore. Aseem took a deep breath. 'It's about Atul,' he began, trying to keep his voice steady. 'He ... he's fine ... but he is not ...'

The floodgates opened. Questions poured out from Anand and Tulsi, their worry evident in every word. *Why hadn't Atul called? Was he really okay? What was going on?*

Aseem wondered how to tell them enough and yet not make them panic. 'He is not okay,' he blurted out, his voice cracking. 'Meaning he is fine, nothing has happened ...'

'Speak clearly now! What happened?' his father's booming command blew away the rest of Aseem's resistance.

'He sent me a message. He says he's being held against his will and forced to work for some bad people.'

The room fell silent. Tulsi's hand flew to her mouth, stifling a sob. Anand's face paled, his hands gripping the edge of the bed. 'What do you mean ... what bad people? How can he ... who is forcing ...' Anand could not even complete his sentence.

'I don't understand everything, but these bad people cheat others for money,' Aseem said, trying to make sense of it while struggling himself. 'Atul said he can't leave. They're making him work for them. But he is okay . . . meaning physically.'

Tulika moved to comfort her parents, her own eyes brimming with tears. 'We'll figure this out,' she said softly, though uncertainty tinged her voice.

Aseem, feeling the need to offer some hope, added, 'Atul sent me details of the agent who arranged his job. I will meet him tomorrow and get more information.'

Anand nodded slowly, his mind reeling with worry. Tulsi began to pray quietly, her lips moving in silent implorations.

4

'Don't these two slides need to be swapped? I think they do.' Radhika said to Jayesh, squinting at his laptop screen. Empty coffee cups and half-eaten sandwiches littered the desk between her and Jayesh. Outside their office window, a billboard advertising a food delivery company twinkled.

'Father loves his numbers,' Jayesh sighed adjusting his collar. 'We should lead with the cost-saving figures?'

'Hmm . . . okay.' Radhika glanced at him. In the past two weeks, she had learned to read the signs. 'Need a break?'

'That obvious?' He attempted a smile.

'You've been opening your shirt button every thirty seconds.'

'It's just . . .' he stood up and began pacing. 'He has such expectations. You know why I was abroad all these years?'

Radhika shook her head, pushing away from the laptop.

'Business school was the official reason. But in reality, I was running away. Panic attacks started in college. Father's . . . disappointments fuelled it more.' He stopped by the window.

'My father is an auto driver,' Radhika said quietly. 'He has worked really hard to educate his four children in the hope that we would have better lives. And here I am, nearing thirty, unmarried, making cold calls to rude customers.' She let out a bitter laugh. 'Want to switch?'

'You have a great future. You're amazing at what you do,' Jayesh turned from the window and looked at her.

Just then his phone rang. The colour drained from his face as he listened.

'What? But we have a contract . . .' His voice tightened. 'When did they . . . yes . . . I understand.'

'What happened?' Radhika stood up.

'Pioneer Suppliers. They're pulling out.' He started pacing again, his fingers working frantically at his collar button. 'It means stop of work . . . delays . . . Fuck!'

'Is it because Gautam is out?

'Father's presentation is tomorrow . . .' Jayesh's breathing became shallow, his words coming faster. 'Whatever timeline and projections we put means nothing now.'

'Hey,' Radhika moved to him, 'it only means they were in it with Gautam. Calm down.' But Jayesh was already sliding down the wall, gasping for air.

Radhika knelt beside him. 'Look at me.' When he didn't respond, she gently took his hand. 'Breathe with me, okay? In . . . and out.'

'Can't . . .' his voice came out choked.

Without thinking, she pressed his hand to her chest. 'Breathe with me. Like this.' His breathing started to even out, matching her rhythm.

'Listen,' she said softly, not moving her hand from his. 'Maybe this is good.' She meant the supplier pulling out.

'It is . . .' His voice was barely a whisper. He meant the breathing.

'If Gautam and Pioneer Suppliers were together . . . as it looks now . . .' she left the implication hanging for a moment. 'I think we might have accidentally solved another problem.' She smiled. 'We'll find new suppliers. Better ones. Trust me?'

Gradually, his breathing steadied. He was still holding her hand. She turned to explain further and found herself staring directly into his eyes. She could feel his breath on her cheek . . .

A sharp whistle from the street below shattered the moment.

'I . . . I should go,' Radhika stepped back, gathering her things with shaking hands. 'It's late.'

'Right,' Jayesh ran a hand through his hair. 'Yes. I'll take a look at the presentation again, but we will go with this then.'

'Good. We will find a supplier.'

At the door, she paused. 'Jayesh?'

'Yes?'
'You're amazing too.'
She left before he could respond, her heart hammering.

5

When Radhika stepped into her home that night, the atmosphere was heavy with an unfamiliar tension. Her parents' bedroom door was closed, but she could hear her mother's muffled sobs.

'Something terrible has happened.' Tulika whispered and started crying.

'What?' Radhika held her sister by the arms. 'Tell me!'

'Atul's job was a scam. He is being held against his will, somewhere in Cambodia.' Aseem broke the terrible news for the third time that day.

Radhika's bag slipped from her shoulder to the floor. Her mother's sobs suddenly seemed to grow louder. The warm glow she had carried home from work was replaced by a dark shadow. She tried to process all that Aseem was saying and just nodded when he said he was going to talk to the agent.

'Have you both eaten?' The words came automatically, her feet already moving toward the kitchen. It was what their mother always did in a crisis—feed everyone.

The untouched food in the kitchen told its own story. She mechanically began heating the rotis. They needed strength for whatever was coming.

Her phone rang almost on cue. It was one of the site workers.

'Madam, come quickly. I have proof of all the wrong-doing.'

Radhika's grip tightened around the phone. 'At this time? It can't wait for morning?'

'No madam, you need to see this now.' His voice was insistent.

'Stay there. I'm coming.' She kept her voice neutral even as her mind raced through the possibilities. The earlier threats, the missing documents and now this convenient late-night revelation.

'Where are you going now?' Tulika asked, hovering in the kitchen doorway.

'Nowhere.' Radhika turned back to the stove, her jaw clenched.

'Who was it?' Aseem asked.

'Just some dimwit trying to be too smart.'

The three siblings ate in silence afterwards. Everyone trying to make sense of what had happened.

6

The next day, Aseem made his way to the address Atul had given. Both his anger and anxiety had been building since he got the messages from Atul. He spotted the board of the placement agency and looked for the entrance. It was a basement office. Aseem quickly climbed down the steps, took a deep breath and burst through the door. The eyes of the middle-aged man sitting behind the desk widened briefly before settling into a practiced mask of neutrality.

'Ah, you seem to be in a hurry young man. Where can I send you?' Sharma's voice was smooth, almost soothing.

Aseem's fists clenched at his sides. 'Are you R.K. Sharma?

Sharma noticed the clenched fists. 'Why are you so agitated? Have a seat, drink some water.' He pressed a switch on his table and a bell rang outside.

'What have you done with my brother? He was supposed to join a company in Bangkok but he is in Cambodia. Why is he being held against his wishes?'

'Does he have a name? Your brother.'

Aseem didn't like the agent's tone. He felt like slapping him.

'His name is Atul Anand. Do you need help in remembering?' Aseem restrained himself to the best he could.

Sharma's eyebrows furrowed in a display of trying to recall. 'Atul? Oh yes . . . I remember now. He called me from Bangkok airport saying he was being sent to Cambodia for training. Is there a problem with his placement?'

'Don't play smart with me,' Aseem's restrain was being tested. He leaned over the desk. 'I got messages from him yesterday, after no news for two weeks. He's being forced to work against his will by some scammers. And he is not allowed to leave. You sent him there!'

Sharma leaned back in his chair, a picture of calm. 'I simply helped your brother secure a job opportunity abroad. What happens after that is beyond my control.'

'I don't believe you,' Aseem said flatly. 'You know exactly what's going on. And if you don't tell me, I'm going straight to the police.'

For a moment, Sharma's composure cracked. A flash of worry crossed his face before he regained control. 'The police? You are free to go to the police. I assure you, I've done nothing wrong.'

Aseem felt a hollowness in his stomach, but he had to press on with his bluff. 'Really? I will go right now. My friend's father is in the Kalkaji thana, I'm sure he would be very interested in hearing about your "job placement" services.'

Aseem turned to go. He could feel Sharma's eyes on him. He had to be convincing. He pushed open the glass panelled door. A boy had just come holding a tray with a glass of water. They almost collided.

'Wait,' Sharma called from behind, his voice losing its smooth edge. 'Let's not be hasty. I . . . I can make some inquiries on your behalf.'

Aseem turned around. 'First, tell me. What do you know about where Atul is?'

Sharma sighed, shoulders slumping slightly. 'I don't know specifics, I swear. But . . . I will check with my contacts to find out.'

'And why should I trust you?' Aseem demanded.

'Because,' Sharma said, meeting Aseem's gaze, 'I am just a middleman, doing a job. I don't want any trouble.'

Aseem studied Sharma's face, searching for any sign of deception. He couldn't tell. Yet, it was a start.

'Fine,' Aseem said, his voice hard. 'But if I find out you're lying or stalling, I won't hesitate to go to the police.'

Sharma nodded, reaching for his phone. 'I understand you. I will make some calls. Let's see what I can find out about your brother's situation.'

Aseem knew he should not trust this man, but there was no other option.

7

Tulika sat reclined on the bed, her back against the wall and her bent knees supporting the thick general studies guidebook. This was her favourite position while studying at home. The house seemed quieter than usual, even though the outside noises were as much as any other day. She hoped Aseem would bring some positive news from the agent. Thankfully her mother had eaten a little bit this morning. Her father had left for work late after ensuring that she ate. *She would most probably be praying in front of her little temple.* Tulika glanced at the calendar on the wall, the date of the UPSC preliminary exam circled in red under the month of May served as a constant reminder.

She picked up a notebook and opened her study schedule, a grid that mapped out every hour of her day until the exam. She was supposed to be studying Indian polity and the Constitution for Paper I right now, followed by exercises from logical reasoning for Paper II after lunch. But her mind kept drifting to Atul's situation.

'Focus, Tulika,' she muttered to herself, pinching the bridge of her nose. 'You can't afford to fail again.'

Last year's failure had been a blow not just to her confidence, but to her father's hopes. She could still remember the disappointment in his eyes, quickly masked by encouragement. 'Next time, beta,' he had said. But she knew what was left unsaid—their family needed this. They needed her to succeed.

Her mother poked her head into the room. 'Do you want some chai, chhoti?'

Tulika forced a smile. 'No, ma. I'm fine.'

As her mother left, Tulika's gaze fell on her phone. There were messages from Amit and Priyal, her study partners. She had messaged them that she would be studying at home for the next few days and they wanted to know if everything was okay. She remembered the way conversations between Amit and Priyal would abruptly change when she approached, the meaningful glances they exchanged.

She shook her head, pushing thoughts of Amit aside. 'Not now,' she whispered. 'I can't deal with that right now.'

Instead, she opened her browser, fingers typing 'Job Scam Cambodia' before she could stop herself. She opened a news article from the search results. It was written by a Nitesh Mishra and described how Indian people who become targets of a foreign job scam end up in 'slave scam compounds' spread across Myanmar, Laos and Cambodia where they were forced to do online scams. People with good spoken English and knowledge of computers were the main targets, Nitesh had written. She went on to another one of his articles. It seemed Nitesh Mishra had written a series of articles on the scams, where not only the people who lost money but even those who conned them were victims. In another article, some people who were lucky to have been rescued shared their traumatic experiences—how they were beaten and kept without food or water when they refused to be involved in the scam operations. She felt scared, imagining Atul in those conditions.

'Tuli,' Aseem's voice broke through her concentration. Aseem was the only person younger to her in this house and he had made his own name for her.

'How did it go with the agent?' Tulika asked.

Aseem's chest puffed up slightly. 'Oh, you should have seen me, I got through his act pretty quickly.'

'What do you mean?'

'Well,' Aseem began, settling on the edge of her bed, 'at first, he tried to act smart, said he didn't know anything about Atul being in trouble. But I wasn't buying it.'

'What happened?' Tulika wanted him to tell her what was important, but Aseem was not going to skip his part.

A smirk played on Aseem's lips. 'I threatened to go to the police. You should have seen how he changed his tune. He has promised to find out what happened and where he is.'

Tulika frowned. 'Do you think he will help?'

Aseem's bravado faltered slightly. Inside he knew that this was just a small first step, but he wanted to be hopeful for himself and for his family. 'I . . . I think so. I will be after him.'

'I might also have found something that could help us,' Tulika said, showing him the open browser on her phone. 'I was doing some research and I came across these articles by someone named Nitesh Mishra.'

Aseem's eyes widened as he scanned the screen. 'You think this guy can help us?'

Tulika nodded, her voice gaining enthusiasm. 'He might have connections that could help us. At least we could find out more.'

'But how do we reach him?'

'He has given his email address and social media handles here. I will contact him.' Tulika scrolled to the bottom of the article.

Aseem's face lit up with hope as Tulika began typing an email to Nitesh Mishra.

8

They sat nervously in the bustling coffee shop in Connaught Place, their eyes darting to the entrance every few seconds. Nitesh Mishra had replied promptly to Tulika's mail and had shared his number too. Now, one day later they were here, hoping the journalist could help them in some way.

'There he is,' Tulika whispered, spotting a man in his mid-forties walking towards them. Nitesh had a weary look about him, but his eyes were sharp and alert. She stood up and waved.

'Tulika?' he asked, extending his hand. She nodded, taking his hand.

As they settled into their seats, Aseem spoke first. 'Sir, I am Aseem. Our brother, Atul—'

'Please, call me Nitesh,' the journalist interrupted gently. 'Now, tell me everything.'

Tulika and Aseem took turns explaining the situation, from Atul's job offer to his message. Nitesh listened intently, his brow furrowing deeper with each detail.

'And you say he mentioned being forced to work, not allowed to leave?' Nitesh asked, leaning forward.

Aseem nodded vigorously. 'Yes, and something about scamming people.'

Nitesh's face darkened. 'I'm afraid this sounds all too familiar. Your brother may be trapped in what I call a "scam compound".'

Tulika gasped. 'Like the ones you wrote about?'

'Yes,' Nitesh confirmed grimly. 'These compounds in countries like Cambodia, Laos and Myanmar are mostly run by Chinese criminals where they force people to carry out online scams.'

Aseem's hands fidgeted nervously on the table. 'How do we get him out?'

Nitesh sighed. 'It's not easy, but I'll assist in any way I can. I know a cybercrime officer who might be able to help us. I will arrange a meeting.'

Aseem's phone buzzed. He glanced at the screen. It was from Sharma.

'I need to take this,' Aseem said and went out.

'Look, these scams have become very sophisticated and convincing. Anybody could get caught in them. I, being a journalist, could not figure out when it happened to me,' Nitesh told Tulika.

'Did you get your money back?' Tulika had read Nitesh's account of his digital arrest and she couldn't stop herself from asking.

'Police were able to block some accounts, so I will get part of it. I was quick to register a complaint. There is a national cybercrime portal and a helpline number for that." Nitesh explained.

Aseem returned and, looking at him, Tulika understood that they had to leave.

'Thank you so much for meeting us, sir,' Tulika said earnestly.

Nitesh stood up. 'It's nothing. Keep me updated. Meanwhile, I'll set up that meeting with the cybercrime officer.'

Aseem, already halfway to the door, said. 'We will. Thanks again!'

9

Radhika found Jayesh lying flat on his back in the middle of his office, arms and legs spread out like a starfish.

'At least it's not headstands today,' she said, closing the door behind her. 'How bad was it?'

'Surprisingly, not terrible.' He didn't move from his position on the floor. 'Father was . . . well, Father. But he has approved the budget revisions. Though he made it very clear that fixing the supplier situation is entirely on me.'

'Us,' Radhika corrected, sitting cross-legged beside him. 'It's on us.'

Jayesh turned his head to look at her, a soft smile playing on his lips. 'What would I do without you?'

'Hmm . . . headstands in client meetings?'

Their laughter filled the room, a reminder of the familiar comfort that had developed between them over the past weeks. Radhika also knew speculation and whispers had already begun circulating about them in the office. It didn't bother her.

'By the way,' Jayesh sat up, 'I filed a police complaint against Gautam after the phone call to you.'

'You didn't have to do that because of me,' Radhika exclaimed. 'I can handle these situations.'

'I know you can. But you shouldn't have to.' He sat leaning against the wall and pulled his knees to his chest. His face looked so vulnerable that Radhika's heart tingled. She remembered him talking about family pressures and his struggle with panic attacks. In that moment she wanted to cradle his head and shoulder his burdens.

'You know, sometimes I wish I could just . . . be honest. Talk freely about everything . . .' He took a deep breath.

'I don't know about others, but you can tell me anything you want to.' Radhika waited for Jayesh to continue but he seemed to be struggling. He needs encouragement, she thought.

'Look, we all have problems. My brother Atul, the one I told you has got a foreign job? Looks like the job was a scam.' The worry that she had forced to the back of her mind finally found an outlet. 'He's in trouble . . . being held somewhere in Cambodia . . .'

Jayesh's expression changed from vulnerability to concern.

'What? When did you find out?' He stood up, what he wanted to talk about forgotten.

'The night we were working on the presentation. We don't know exactly what's happening, but . . .' She felt her voice crack slightly.

Jayesh moved closer, placing a hand on her shoulder. 'Whatever you need, whatever I can do to help . . .'

His phone buzzed—his father's name flashing on the screen. Jayesh glanced at it, then back at Radhika. 'I have to go see my father. But we'll talk about your brother later.'

Only after he left a realization struck Radhika. He had wanted to say something important and she had stopped him.

10

Aseem and Tulika rushed into Sharma's office, their faces flushed from the hurried journey from Connaught Place.

'What did you find . . .?' Aseem asked even before they sat in front of Sharma.

Sharma looked surprised to see another person and glanced at Aseem with a questioning expression.

'This is my sister Tulika . . . How is Atul?'

'It wasn't easy, but I've made contact with the people holding your brother,' Sharma said, feeling reassured by Aseem's answer.

'What did they say?' Aseem asked, his voice tense.

Sharma sighed, rubbing his forehead. 'They're willing to release him, but . . . they want money.'

'How much?' Aseem leaned forward, hope flickering in his eyes.

'I managed to negotiate it down,' Sharma said, putting a note of importance in his voice. 'They initially wanted much more, but I got them to agree to this.' He took out a piece of paper and put it in front of them. It had twenty thousand dollars scribbled on it.

The siblings exchanged a look of disbelief. Tulika's face paled as she did the mental math.

'That's . . . how much . . . 16–17 lakhs . . . that's too . . .' Tulika stammered. 'We don't have that kind of money.'

'I understand it's not little,' Sharma replied, his tone softening. 'But believe me, it was difficult enough to get in touch with them, let alone negotiate. This is the best deal we're going to get.'

Tulika slumped in her chair, her face ashen. 'We can't . . . How are we supposed to come up with that much?'

Aseem ran a hand through his hair, frustration etched on his face. 'There has to be another way. Can't you negotiate further?'

'I'm sorry, but this is it,' Sharma said firmly, spreading his hands. 'They won't budge any lower. It's either this or . . . well, they say Atul has to earn that much plus his daily expenses by working out there.'

The weight of the situation pressed down on Aseem and Tulika. Aseem had begun to realize that Sharma was too cunning to be scared by his threat of going to the police. All the hope they had built up over the past couple of days seemed to evaporate in an instant.

'That's not fair. They are keeping him illegally . . . and now they're asking for money . . . This is ransom,' Aseem spoke up, his voice rising with frustration.

'I don't know what to say. I did whatever I could,' Sharma replied, his expression unreadable.

'You're the one who put him in this situation in the first place,' Aseem accused, standing up abruptly.

Tulika placed a calming hand on Aseem's arm. 'We'll . . . we'll figure something out,' she said, her voice trembling. 'Thank you for the information, Sharma ji. We'll be in touch.'

They left Sharma's office and Tulika sat down, leaning against a wall, her head in her hands. 'What are we going to do, Aseem? We can't possibly raise that much money.'

Aseem squatted beside her, his own despair mirroring hers. 'I don't know, Tuli. I really don't know.'

The siblings sat there on the pavement, the enormity of the problem looming over them like a dark cloud. The glimmer of hope they had felt had been replaced by a crushing sense of helplessness.

11

Nitesh Mishra guided Aseem, Tulika and Anand through the corridors of the police building. The Anand family's nervousness was palpable as they approached DCP Gurnam Singh's office.

'Nitesh ji! Good to see you again,' the officer greeted cheerfully and shook hands with Nitesh as they entered. DCP Singh, in his early forties, cut an imposing figure, his navy blue turban neatly tied above a face framed by a salt-and-pepper beard. A slight paunch pushed against his uniform, but he exuded an air of authority. He did a polite namaste to the rest of them. 'And this must be the boy's family. Please, sit down.' He gestured to the chairs in front of his desk.

Anand lowered himself onto a chair, his calloused hands fidgeting in his lap. 'Yes, sir. We've come about my son.'

DCP Singh leaned forward, his expression turning serious. 'Nitesh ji briefed me over the phone, but I would like to hear directly from you. Tell me whatever you know.'

'Atul went to join a job in Bangkok. After that we could not contact him . . . what happened, sahab . . . I . . . don't under . . .' Anand started to choke.

'He contacted me a few days ago. Around two weeks after he'd left,' Aseem picked up. As they took turns to narrate everything since Atul had left, DCP Singh made some notes.

'I must say, this is new for Delhi,' he remarked after they had finished.

'What do you mean, sir?' Tulika asked softly, her eyes wide with concern.

'Well,' Singh began, stroking his beard thoughtfully, 'I am aware of similar job trafficking cases from Andhra and Tamil Nadu. But this is the first time it has come to light here in Delhi.'

Aseem shifted in his seat, barely containing his anxiousness. 'So, what can you do? How do we get Atul back?'

The DCP sighed, his expression serious. 'I won't sugarcoat things. This will be a long process. We'll need to work with various agencies, including our embassy folks in Cambodia. Cross-border coordination is never easy.'

'Please do whatever you can, sahab. Please bring my son back,' Anand implored with folded hands, his voice trembling.

Singh folded his hands in empathy with a grieving father. 'I am telling you this because you will need to stay strong. These compounds are apparently scattered across remote areas, making it difficult for their police to find what we are looking for. But I promise you that I will make every effort.'

Anand once again folded his hands. This time in gratitude.

'First steps first. We'll start by registering a case,' he said picking up the intercom. A junior officer came almost immediately. 'Bakshi, please assist them with filing a case and discuss it with me later.'

'Tell him all that you know,' DCP Singh told Anand.

As the SI led the family out, the DCP called out. 'Send tea for Nitesh ji!'

'So, Nitesh ji,' Singh said with a wry smile, 'Getting digitally arrested is coming to some use.'

Nitesh grimaced. 'Don't remind me, sir. I still can't believe how I fell for it.'

'Well, at least some good came out of it,' Singh replied, his tone turning serious. 'Your articles have been invaluable in raising awareness. Keep writing.'

12

Back in their home, the family kept discussing what DCP Singh's words meant. On the one hand, there was a hope that a case was registered and the police would be looking for Atul. But on the other hand, there was also the stark reality of a long and uncertain wait.

'So, what do we do now?' Anand's voice was a tired whisper, not saying it to anyone in particular and yet to everyone, his gaze fixed on a damp patch on the wall above their heads.

Before anyone could answer, Aseem's phone pinged loudly, attracting glances from his sisters. He took it out from his pant pocket. It was a message from Ravi: 'Time's running out, bro. Need that money ASAP.'

Tulika reached out and squeezed her father's hand. 'We wait, papa. The police will find bhaiya.'

'We can't just sit and wait,' Aseem spoke in a sudden burst. 'The DCP himself said it could take forever and still he may not be found. There is only one sure way, we pay for his release.'

Anand sighed, rubbing his forehead. 'But that much money is impossible.'

A loud sob escaped Tulsi even as she tried to stop it, her saree clutched in her mouth. Anand helplessly looked at his wife and bowed his head down.

'Let's put together everything that we can. I have about fifty thousand.' Aseem pushed through his line of thought.

Radhika stopped pacing and turned to face her family. 'I can ask for an advance from my office. It won't be much, but let's say about one and a half to two lakhs.' She was counting on Jayesh to come good on his promise of help.

'I will take a loan against the auto. And there is the saving that I kept for Radhika's marriage.' Anand spoke like a broken man.

'Don't worry about the marriage, papa. But still all of this won't be more than seven lakhs. What will that do against the demand of almost 17 lakhs?'

'I will make the agent renegotiate,' Aseem spoke as if he was seeing things clearly.

'How?' Radhika questioned.

Aseem shrugged. 'I don't know . . . but it's our best chance,' he said.

Radhika looked at Aseem, her eyes narrowed in suspicion. 'I hope there is nothing else going on in your head. Haven't you been begging papa for money for your stupid gym?'

'What rubbish are you talking? I have given up on that!' Aseem said defensively.

Anand looked at his son with a strange mix of hope and doubt. 'If there's any chance, any at all, I'll give every last rupee I have.'

Aseem looked at his father, then his mother. His gaze lingering, he thought, *This was now or never. He had to do it.*

Seven

1

ASEEM LEFT THE HOUSE AFTER the family discussion during which they had decided to collect all the money they could for Atul's release. Before leaving, he had assured them that he would renegotiate the ransom through the agent. Since then, he hadn't returned their calls and had only sent occasional messages that he was on it. And now, on the third night, Aseem walked in and announced. 'They've . . . they've agreed to a lower amount.'

Radhika's head snapped up, her eyes narrowing with suspicion. 'How much?'

Aseem swallowed hard before answering. 'What do you mean how much? To what we have!'

A collective gasp filled the room. Tulsi suddenly had a smile on her face almost after three weeks and ran to her room to thank her gods. Anand let out a sigh of relief and, looking up, clasped his palms together, saying a silent prayer.

'Are you sure, beta? This isn't some trick?' Anand asked.

Radhika looked at everyone present, wondering how they were not seeing the obvious connection. This was what Aseem needed to open his gym.

'So, basically, they agreed on the amount that we told you we can collect. How?' Radhika questioned.

Aseem nodded his head vigorously. 'Yes. I told them that this is all we have. And that Atul can never be useful to them because he cannot scam anyone even if he tries to. They have realized it themselves by now.'

Radhika paced the small room, her brow furrowed in thought. She couldn't shake the feeling that something was off. 'And how exactly do we pay this money? How can we be sure they'll release Atul?'

Aseem turned to look at his father, away from Radhika. 'I will give the money to the agent. He will send it to them. They'll let Atul go after that.'

'Just like that?' Radhika scoffed. 'This seems too convenient.'

'The agent is the guarantor. He is not going anywhere,' Aseem tried to reassure everyone.

Tulika, who had been quiet until now, spoke up. 'What other choice do we have? This is a chance to bring bhaiya home . . .'

Anand nodded slowly, making his decision. He looked at each of his children.

'We'll do it,' Anand said, his voice gaining strength. 'We'll pay the money.'

Radhika opened her mouth to say something but then stopped. She looked at her father, then her brother, and said, 'Okay. I will get the money tomorrow. You better not be lying to us.'

Anand looked at his youngest son, seeing not the troublemaker or the dreamer, but a man stepping up for his family. 'Bring your brother home, Aseem,' he said softly. 'Bring our Atul back to us.'

Aseem nodded and shut his eyes hiding the tears that welled up in his eyes. A sense of unease weighed on him thinking about what he was going to do. *They wouldn't have given me the money if they knew.*

2

Aseem met Ravi at their usual spot, a roadside tea shop near the gym.

Ravi was leaning against his motorcycle, having tea from a small disposable cup. As Aseem stopped his bike near him, he asked in a somewhat uncertain tone, 'You got it?'

Aseem nodded and without getting off the bike handed over a folded polythene bag.

Ravi unfolded the bag and opened it slightly to peek inside at the bundles of cash. 'Aseem, are you sure about this? There's no going back, you understand?' Ravi looked up, studying his friend's face.

Aseem felt a dark fear rise inside him. He clenched his jaws. 'Yes, I understand. Let's just get it over with.'

3

Radhika almost cancelled the lunch. With everything happening at home, sitting in a fancy restaurant felt wrong, selfish. But something in Jayesh's voice when he called in the morning made her come. Perhaps, she thought, she needed one normal conversation away from worried faces and discussions about ransom money.

She stepped into the hotel's fine-dining restaurant, her cotton kurti feeling suddenly inadequate among the weekend crowd in their designer wear. She spotted Jayesh at a corner table, already nursing what looked like a whiskey.

'You're drinking at lunch?' she asked, sliding into the chair across from him. The elegant table setting and soft classical music seemed at odds with his dishevelled appearance.

'Bad morning with my father.' He attempted a smile that didn't reach his eyes. 'Thank you for coming on such short notice.'

A waiter appeared with a repeat of Jayesh's drink.

'Do you want something to drink?' Jayesh asked.

'I'm good with water.' Radhika smiled.

'Wait for me to call you.' Jayesh dismissed the waiter impatiently.

'What happened with your father?' Radhika asked, trying to focus on him despite her exhaustion from a sleepless night.

He took a long sip before answering. 'He's planning this grand celebration for my thirtieth birthday in June. The whole family will be there—uncles, aunts, cousins from everywhere.' He laughed bitterly. 'He's been telling everyone there'll be a special announcement.'

'Oh.' Radhika's heart quickened.

'He's given me an ultimatum. Either I choose someone, or he will.' Jayesh's fingers drummed nervously on the table. One of them was having trouble breathing. For a change, it wasn't Jayesh. *Was this leading where she thought it might?*

'Have you found that someone?' Radhika couldn't resist asking.

'There's something I need to tell you, Radhika. Something I've never told anyone here.'

She leaned forward, the troubles at home momentarily forgotten. 'What is it?'

'In the US, I was in a relationship.' He paused, swirling the amber liquid in his glass. 'With my professor.'

Radhika smiled slightly. 'Boys and their thing for older female teachers.'

'He wasn't a woman.' Jayesh was speaking in whispers. 'Brad was . . . is his name.'

The world seemed to tilt on its axis. Radhika gripped the edge of the table, her mind racing back through every interaction, every moment she had thought held special meaning.

'I . . . I don't understand. Why are you telling me this now?'

'Because I trust you. And because I have a proposition.' He leaned forward, lowering his voice. 'Marry me.'

Radhika jerked back as if struck. 'What?'

'Listen, please. It could work perfectly. You know who I am now, there would be no expectations, no pressure. You would have complete freedom to live your life, even have other relationships if you want. I can provide financial security and you can continue your career without family pressure about marriage.'

'Are you serious?' Radhika's voice cracked. 'You're proposing a sham marriage? After everything we've—' She stopped, realizing there was no 'we' to speak of.

'It's not a sham. It's a modern arrangement between friends who understand each other. You're the only person I trust with this, Radhika. The only one who would understand.'

'Understand?' She stood up abruptly, her chair scraping against the floor. A waiter approached but retreated at Radhika's expression. 'Understand that you've been letting me . . . letting everyone think . . .' Her voice trembled with hurt and anger.

'Radhika, please . . .'

'I need to go.' She grabbed her bag, barely holding back tears. 'Don't follow me.'

As she hurried through the restaurant, past the curious glances of other diners, she couldn't decide what hurt more—the death of her unspoken hopes, or the realization that, to Jayesh, she was just a convenient solution to his problem.

4

The small, windowless room had become Atul's world for the past week. The stench of his own body and the urine he had to pass in one corner completed the humiliation.

On top of that, the claustrophobia of the cramped space and the constant semi darkness pressed in on him from all sides. The single daily meal and brief toilet break were his only connections to the outside world. Altogether, both his body and soul were weakened.

As the door opened, Atul's heart raced with a desperate hope. The guards shoved a plate of unappetising looking sticky rice. Though he was very hungry, he ignored the food and cried out in a hoarse voice, 'Please, I need a bath. Just let me clean myself.'

The guards' laughter echoed off the bare walls. 'Look at the prince, wanting a bath!' one sneered in broken English. 'You smell like pig, it suits you!'

Before Atul could say anything more, a hand shoved him back. He fell in the corner of the floor wet with urine. Curled up on the ground, in his own piss, the last shreds of dignity and resistance crumbled away from him. 'I'll do it,' he whispered, his voice barely audible. 'I'll do whatever you want. Just . . . please.'

The guard about to shut the door paused. 'What was that, pig?'

Atul pushed himself up to his knees, his eyes downcast. 'I said I'll do it. I'll do whatever I am told. Whatever the manager says. Just . . . let me out of here.'

'I will tell the boss. Let me see what he says.' The Chinese guard sneered and slammed the door shut, leaving Atul once again in darkness.

5

The WhatsApp message was simple: *Come down for 2 minutes. Please.*

Soni checked the time, 12.22 AM, and typed furiously: *Are you crazy?*

Completely. About you.

She couldn't help smiling. *Cheezy haan!*

Come down na. Just 2 minutes. Promise.

Soni quickly threw a dupatta over her night dress and ran her fingers through her messy hair. She tiptoed out of her house only to find Aseem standing under the street light imitating Bollywood icon Shah Rukh Khan's famous 'arms spread' pose.

'Stop that,' she whispered, suppressing a laugh. 'Do you know what time it is?'

'I missed you,' Aseem said with his trademark grin, but something seemed off. 'Isn't this romantic?'

'Romantic? My father will kill you if he—'

'Then let's run away,' he interrupted, still grinning but not quite meeting her eyes.

'Aseem, what's wrong?'

'Wrong? Nothing's wrong. Everything's right. Or will be.' He ran his hand through his hair. 'I just . . . I have to go away for some time.'

'Go away? Where?'

'I have some work to do.' He took her hand, and she felt it trembling slightly. 'It is about the gym.' He added rather hastily.

'You are not getting into any trouble, are you?'

'Trouble? Me?' He placed a hand on his chest in mock offence. 'I'm the trouble-solver of Mandawali. The solution-provider of Patparganj. The—'

'Aseem.'

He stopped, looked at her for a long moment.

'When will you come back?'

'I don't know exactly.'

'That's no answer.'

'Listen,' Aseem said quickly, 'I need you to have faith in me. Just this once.'

'You're scaring me.'

'Don't be scared.' He grinned, but his eyes were serious. '*Main hoon na?*'

'Did you really just quote Shah Rukh Khan?'

'Hey, if one is trying to have a last-minute romantic conversation, might as well steal from the best.'

'Last-minute?' Soni's eyes narrowed. 'When are you leaving?'

'Soon.' He glanced at his watch. 'But I'll be back before you know it. And then I'll take you to a fancy restaurant, even if it costs me a month's salary.'

'I don't care about fancy restaurants.'

'I know. And I love you.'

The words hung in the silence of the night. Soni was going to say that she loved him too. But Aseem pulled her close, tilted her face up and kissed her with a sudden force that left her breathless. This wasn't like their usual careful, quick kisses—this was different, desperate almost, like he was trying to keep a part of her with him forever. Soni felt herself melting into him, her hands finding their way to his chest. For a few precious seconds, the world disappeared—no worried fathers, no uncertain futures, just them.

The sudden sweep of headlights from a passing car broke the spell. Soni quickly stepped back into the shadows, her heart racing, lips tingling.

'I should go,' Aseem said, his voice hoarse as he mounted his bike.

'Aseem . . .'

He kicked the starter. 'Have faith in me, okay? Even if . . . even if things seem strange for a while. Promise me?'

Before she could answer, he leaned forward and brushed his lips against hers—gentle now, like the affirmation of a promise. Then he was gone, leaving Soni standing in the dark, her fingers touching her lips where his taste still lingered. He had never been so bold and he had never kissed her like that before. As her racing heart slowly steadied, she realized he hadn't actually answered any of her questions.

6

The small living room of the Anand household seemed to have shrunk as the whole family stood there, each one battling different emotions. Aseem stood in the centre of the room facing it all with downcast eyes, a packed bag at his feet, while his family surrounded him.

He could have left without a word, disappeared into the night. But after what happened with Atul, he couldn't bear to put them through that again. They deserved at least this much—knowing he was leaving by choice.

Anand's voice trembled with barely contained rage. 'Where's your brother, Aseem? You said you have given the money and Atul would be home. Where is he? What are you not telling us!'

Aseem avoided his father's gaze, his usual confidence noticeably absent. 'I'm handling it, papa. These things . . . they take time.'

A muscle twitched in his jaw as he lowered his face even further. Anyone in the room at that moment would have interpreted it as him not being able to look them in the eye, hiding his shame.

Radhika stepped forward, her eyes narrowed with suspicion. 'Enough of your excuses and lies, Aseem. The money's gone into your stupid gym plan, hasn't it?'

Tulsi pleaded in a soft voice. 'Beta, look at me. Tell me you haven't betrayed your own brother.'

'I can't . . . I don't . . .' Aseem mumbled, reaching for his bag. 'I have to leave for a few days,' he added, still not meeting anyone's eyes.

'Leave for where?' Anand's voice had turned cold, a tone Aseem had never heard before. 'After taking everything we had? After giving us false hope about Atul?'

Radhika lunged forward, grabbing Aseem's arm. 'You're not going anywhere until you tell us the truth!'

Aseem wrenched his arm free, a flash of pain crossing his face. 'I have to go. I'm sorry.'

'I never expected much from you. I thought one of my four children has turned out useless, but I could live with that,' Anand said, his voice dropping even lower. 'But someone who will cheat his own family is more like a dangerous disease. From today . . . you're not part of this family!' The last words exploded in a shout that seemed to shake the walls.

A gasp escaped Tulsi, tears spilling down her cheeks. Aseem's fingers dug into the strap of his bag.

Throughout, Tulika had been observing from the corner. Something in Aseem's rigid posture, in the way he kept swallowing as if fighting back words, made her doubt things. 'Aseem,' she said softly, 'what's really going on?'

Aseem's eyes flickered to Tulika for a moment, something indefinable passing across his face. But then he straightened his shoulders, gripped his bag tighter and turned towards the door.

'I have to go,' he said, his voice barely above a whisper.

'Then go!' Anand shouted, his face red with anger. 'And don't you dare come back!'

Aseem paused for a moment at the threshold, turned to look at his crying mother and whispered, 'Sorry, ma.' Without another word, he stepped out, closing the door behind him.

Eight

1

He said a polite thank you to the air hostess and stepped onto the jet bridge. Aseem had been nervous while boarding the aircraft in Delhi and throughout most of the journey. Different scenarios had played in his head. He had feared something bad would happen. But now, those fears were behind him—it was time to face reality. He would know very soon whether he had been right or wrong. Not for nothing had Tulika called him the prince of failed plans. *But this time it has to work*, he told himself as he walked towards the airport terminal.

Three days ago, he had met Ravi at the tea stall and handed him 50,000 rupees—all the money he had. Ravi had asked if he was sure and he had said, 'Let's just get this done with.'

The next day, they kidnapped Sharma.

Aseem, Ravi, and another person whom Ravi had brought in, waited in a car on the opposite side of the road from Sharma's office, a little further down the street. At half past six in the evening, the office boy had left.

Aseem had staked Sharma's office for two days before that and he knew that the office boy was the only other person in there. They waited for him to go out of sight before Ravi drove the car across the street and stopped it just outside the office. There was a lot of movement on the street, but there were no streetlights and it was getting dark. He and the new guy, who insisted on being called Thor, moved quickly into the office. Aseem switched off all the lights while Thor kept Sharma under control with his hammer raised and aimed at his head. Aseem then told Sharma, 'You just need to spend a few days with us. I promise no harm will come to you, and neither will I ask you for money.'

'What do you want?' Sharma had asked.

'I will tell you. Understand one thing clearly. I know your house, I know you have three kids, I know where the elder one plays football, where the younger boy goes to learn guitar and where your little girl's dance classes happen. If you try to act smart now, or anytime before my work is done, I will go and pick one of them. If you cooperate, I will let you go myself.'

There had been no trouble after that.

They had waited in that darkened office until it was ten, just to make sure that there would be less traffic. Then they took Sharma to a house on the Delhi-Gurgaon border that Ravi had arranged. As planned, Ravi and Thor had worn masks in front of Sharma; Aseem saw no point in hiding his own identity.

The immigration queue moved slowly at the Phnom Penh International Airport. Aseem wondered how people like Sharma, who put the lives of others in danger, were so fearful when it was their own turn.

The person ahead of him went to the counter—next would be his turn. He thought back to that night when they had abducted Sharma.

'You understand what you need to do, right?' Aseem had asked in a low but firm voice.

Sharma nodded in agreement but the words that came out from his mouth said that Aseem's plan was not going to work. 'I'll make the call, but they will never agree to this. You are mad to think it will happen. It's impossible.' Sharma was tied to the chair he was sitting on, with rope going around his waist.

Aseem leaned in close, his voice steady and cold. 'Tell them I will expose you to the police if this does not happen. You say whatever you need to make this happen. You put my brother into this, now you make this possible. Or I will bring your children here.'

Sharma's hands shook as he dialled the number. Aseem listened intently.

'I have a new offer from Atul's family,' Sharma said, his voice quavering. 'They have been able to collect 7,000 dollars for the boy's release.'

Something was said from the other side and Sharma replied, 'That's all the money they have.'

There was a longer pause. The person on the other side of the call shouted some reply. Aseem held his breath.

'No, wait!' Sharma pleaded. 'There's one more thing . . .'

The conversation went back and forth for a while. Aseem waited, filled with anxiety but not showing it.

Sharma didn't speak for a moment after the call ended. He just slumped in the chair, despite being tied. His head dropped to his chest. Aseem feared the worst. Then, Sharma looked up with relief flooding his eyes and said, 'It's done. They have agreed.'

'Next,' called the immigration officer. Aseem stepped forward. He handed over his passport, praying silently that everything would go smoothly.

The officer looked at the passport, then at Aseem. 'Purpose of your visit to Cambodia?'

'Tourist,' he replied.

As the officer stamped his passport, Aseem felt relief. He was in. Just one more step now.

Aseem walked through the exit gate pulling his small trolley bag along. He stopped when he reached the drop area for the departures. While waiting at the Delhi airport earlier, he had watched many videos of this place to familiarize himself. It still felt different. He had to wait now. He kept looking here and there, searching for his brother.

2

Aseem stood outside the departure gate of the airport, scanning the incoming crowd for almost half an hour. He started to lose hope. Then, he saw them: Atul and three other men walking towards him. Aseem's breath caught in his throat at the sight of his brother, who looked thin and haggard.

As the group approached, Aseem steeled himself. He pulled out an envelope containing $7000 from his small belt pouch and held it out. The burly security chief eyed him suspiciously before snatching the envelope and quickly counting its contents.

Satisfied with the amount, Kovac nodded to his men. One of the guards pushed Atul forward, while the other handed him his passport. Atul stumbled, clearly disoriented by the sight of his brother and the turn of events.

Aseem quickly pulled out a ticket, the money left from what his father had given him and a mobile phone. 'Here,' he said, pressing them into Atul's hands. 'All the necessary contacts are in the phone. My date of birth is the password. Go inside the airport now.'

Atul blinked in confusion, his eyes darting between Aseem and the guards. 'But what about—'

'Just go, bhaiya,' Aseem interrupted firmly. 'I am coming.'

Still bewildered, Atul did as he was told. He turned to look at the departure gate and Aseem waved, signalling him to keep going. Once he was inside, Atul again looked back, expecting to see Aseem following him. Instead, he watched in shock as his brother began walking in the opposite direction.

Aseem strode purposefully with Kovac ahead of him and the guards close behind. Without hesitation, he followed the men into a waiting vehicle and the door slammed shut behind him. As the SUV pulled away from the curb, Aseem caught a glimpse of Atul's stunned face through the airport's glass doors.

Aseem handed over his passport and, even as the guards searched him, leaned back in his seat, closing his eyes. He had done what he needed to do to get his brother out. Now, he would have to make one more plan. It better be good—his life depended on it.

3

Atul stood frozen in disbelief, his eyes fixed in the distance where the SUV carrying Aseem had disappeared. His mind reeled, trying to make sense of what had just happened. The weight of the phone, money and ticket in his hands felt surreal. Did his younger brother exchange himself to secure his freedom just now?

'Aseem . . . what have you done?' he whispered, his voice trembling.

Atul stumbled to a nearby chair and collapsed into it. He stared at the ticket in his hand—the flight to Delhi was in four hours. *I can't go back to India, not without Aseem.* With shaking hands, Atul unlocked the phone and scrolled through the contacts. His finger hovered over the number under 'Home', but he couldn't bring himself to call. Instead, he stood up, a new determination settling over him.

Atul approached the information desk, his voice steadier than he felt. 'Excuse me, I need to speak with the airport manager. It's urgent.'

The staff member looked at him curiously but nodded, directing him to an office nearby. Atul knocked on the door, and after a brief wait, he was ushered in.

'How can I help you, sir?' the manager asked, eyeing Atul's dishevelled appearance with concern.

Atul took a deep breath. 'I need the contact information for the Indian embassy. My . . . someone I know is in some trouble and needs help.'

The manager's expression softened with understanding. 'I will suggest that you look up the embassy website—all details will be there. You can connect to the free Wi-Fi in the airport.'

'Thank you,' Atul looked at the phone in his hand. He had not thought about checking the website in his panicked state. As he turned to leave, he paused at the door. 'One more thing . . . where can I change this ticket to a later date? Or cancel it? I won't be leaving today.'

The manager nodded. 'I'll have someone assist you with that.'

Atul stepped out of the office with a strengthened resolve. He would not abandon Aseem.

4

The stench of cheap perfume mixed with sweat made Radhika's stomach turn. The brutal Delhi summer of May had transformed the interior into a suffocating sauna. Getting crushed between bodies in the overcrowded DTC bus, she tried to find a spot to rest her eyes that wasn't someone else's armpit. A woman's enormous shopping bag kept jabbing into her ribs, while a man's briefcase banged against her knees with every lurch of the bus.

The conductor pushed through, counting notes for someone's change. The mechanical movement of his fingers brought back memories—her father at the dining table, counting out their savings with trembling hands before giving everything to Aseem. Her mother's quiet sobs from the kitchen. Tulika pretending to study but really just staring at the same page for hours.

A sharp elbow dug into her side as someone pushed past to get to the door. Radhika shifted, finding herself face-to-face with a middle-aged man whose eyes lingered shamelessly. This could be her future—daily buses, unwanted stares, living a hopeless life in some cramped flat with a husband who wouldn't be very different from the men around her right now. A life not unlike her parents', except they lived that life with only one dream, that their children would have a better life.

There was Jayesh's offer, of course. His words played in her mind: 'Complete freedom . . . financial security . . . a modern arrangement between friends.' The bus jerked to another stop and more passengers squeezed in. Someone's hand pressed against her back, pushing her forward. No, with Jayesh there would be no love, but there would be respect, independence and most importantly, the means to help her family.

Her phone buzzed in her bag. An email from HR requesting an urgent meeting. Perfect, she thought bitterly, she was probably getting fired for not accepting Jayesh's offer or for spending too much time dealing with a family crisis.

Twenty minutes later, she sat across the HR person, trying to process what she was hearing.

'The top management was particularly impressed with how you handled the site crisis,' HR was saying. 'Mr Jayesh specifically mentioned your problem-solving abilities. We would like to offer you a permanent position as project manager, with a significant raise.'

Radhika stared at the offer letter. The salary figure was more than triple what she currently made. She could help pay off the mortgage her father had taken against his auto, the money that Aseem had swindled. She could support Tulika's UPSC preparation . . .

'I'll need your decision by next week,' HR added.

'I accept,' Radhika said immediately. 'I'll take it.'

Walking to the coffee house later that afternoon, Radhika felt the weight of multiple decisions settling on her shoulders. The cafe was nearly empty at this odd hour between lunch and the evening rush. Jayesh sat at a corner table, fidgeting with his shirt collar. He looked up when she entered, his face a mixture of hope and anxiety.

'You called,' he said softly as she sat down.

'Yes.' She placed her bag on the empty chair beside her. 'I've been thinking about your proposal.'

'And?' His fingers tightened around his shirt's top button.

'I have conditions.' She sat straighter, channelling the same confidence she had used at the construction site. 'First, complete financial transparency. We maintain separate accounts, but we're clear about our expenses.'

He nodded, relief beginning to show in his features.

'Second, separate bedrooms. Non-negotiable.'

'Of course.'

'Third, my career is important to me. I don't want any favours but no interference either.'

'I wouldn't have it any other way.' He managed a small smile. 'You're brilliant at what you do. But not even a suggestion as a friend?'

'We will see. Fourth,' she paused, 'my salary goes into my account. I'll use it for my personal expenses and to support my family. The house expenses—rent, bills, maintenance, everything—that's on you.'

Jayesh nodded. 'That's fair.'

'Fifth,' she leaned forward, her voice hardening, 'if you ever bring someone home, I need to know in advance. I won't be made a fool of in my own house. If anyone finds out about this arrangement, it's my reputation on the line more than yours. You understand that, right?'

The colour drained from his face. 'I would never—'

'And finally,' she leaned forward, making sure he met her eyes, 'we're clear about what this is. A practical arrangement between friends. No mixed signals, no changing the terms later.'

'Absolutely clear.' He reached for his wallet. 'Should we discuss how to tell our families?'

'Not yet.' Radhika held up her hand. 'First, I need to hear you say it. Why me, Jayesh? Really?'

He was quiet for a moment, studying his coffee. 'Because you're the strongest person I know,' he said finally. 'Because you understand duty and family, but you're not bound by conventions. Because . . .' he looked up at her, 'because I trust you with my truth, and I think you trust me . . . I hope you will trust me enough to build something honest, even if it's not traditional.'

'Why can't you just tell your father what you really want? It would be much simpler,' Radhika pressed.

'No. It wouldn't. Not until I can stand on my own.'

Radhika nodded slowly. 'Okay then. Okay. About telling our parents? If your parents are fine with you marrying an auto driver's daughter, I will manage mine.'

Outside, the evening traffic had begun to build up. Through the cafe window, she could see buses crawling past, packed with tired passengers heading home. She had chosen a different path—not better, not worse, just different. Like the promotion letter in her bag, it felt like both an ending and a beginning.

'One more thing,' she turned back to Jayesh, her tone shifting to the same fierce one she had used with Vikram and Gautam. 'If you ever try to play smart with me, I'll make your panic attacks look like a picnic. Clear?'

He laughed. The laugh had a nervous edge to it.

Nine

1

ATUL WALKED THROUGH THE DOORS of the Indian embassy, his clothes rumpled and his eyes wild with desperation. The cool air conditioning made him shudder, but he felt a little relief too. He felt safe. His legs gave up even as he tried to grip the edge of the reception counter for support.

'I need help,' he croaked while collapsing. his voice hoarse from exhaustion. 'My brother . . .'

The receptionist, alarmed by Atul's situation, helped him sit on a sofa and went back to make a call on the intercom. She then brought him a glass of water and helped him drink it. Atul felt better. 'My brother . . . has been taken.' It took him a moment to find the right word.

A middle-aged man with a kind face came in and introduced himself as the second secretary Avinash Kapoor.

'How can I help you?' he said. 'Tell me what's happened.'

Words tumbled out in a frantic rush. Atul recounted his own captivity in the scam compound, the hellish conditions and finally, Aseem's unexpected arrival and what happened after that.

'He . . . he traded places with me,' Atul choked out, tears welling in his eyes. 'My brother gave himself up so I could be free.'

Avinash's expression darkened as he listened. When Atul finished, the official let out a heavy sigh, rubbing his temples.

'Atul,' he said, his voice a mix of sympathy and frustration, 'I understand your distress, but we could have been of help if your brother had informed the embassy earlier. We could have coordinated with local authorities, arranged a police raid during the exchange.'

Atul's face fell. 'I . . . I don't know what he was thinking, sir. Please help.'

As Avinash explained the complexities of international law enforcement and diplomatic channels, Atul's mind raced, imagining Aseem facing the same horrors he had endured—or worse. 'I do understand that he may have done it out of ignorance, but it is also true that we cannot always trust the police. The people running these scamming compounds have deep pockets and deeper connections,' he added.

Suddenly, Atul sat up straighter, a spark of determination in his eyes. 'I spent more than a month in that compound,' he said, his voice growing stronger. 'I don't know where exactly it is, but it is approximately two hours' drive from here. I know the layout, names of people there.'

Mr Kapoor leaned forward. 'That could have some value,' he admitted. 'But you must understand, Mr Anand, this won't be a quick process. We'll need to involve multiple agencies, both here and back in India.'

Atul nodded, his jaw set with resolve. 'I won't leave Cambodia without my brother.'

'Give me your passport. We don't want your visa to expire while you are here,' Mr Kapoor said. Atul handed his passport over. Kapoor then scribbled something on a paper. 'Take this. It is a cheap but good hotel close by. Do you have money?'

'Yes,' Atul said feeling the notes in his pocket that Aseem gave him. It wasn't much but he would think about that later.

'Good! You look like you need a bath and some sleep. Go now and come back tomorrow morning. I will connect with some people in the meantime.'

Atul realized there was nothing else he could do there for now. He did need to eat and sleep.

He thanked the officer and left.

2

Chu's cold eyes bored into Aseem who stood with a wide smile pasted on his face, trying to show that he was unbothered. He had been brought straight to the manager's office upon their arrival—the cold bare room with Chu in his massive chair. Kovac stood behind them, expressionless as always.

'Good evening, sir! Happy to be here!'

'Where is Sharma? Release him now,' Chu ordered, his voice sharp.

Aseem nodded. 'Definitely sir. But if I can, with sincere respect, request one small thing?'

Chu's eyes narrowed. 'Now what?'

'I have to call my brother, just to ensure he boarded the flight safely. To calm my mind, sir.'

The manager's face twisted into a snarl. 'Do not test me, boy. You are here now, and here, I decide.'

Despite the threat in Chu's voice, Aseem maintained his extra polite demeanour. 'Definitely, sir... I understand, sir. You will have no complaints about my work. In fact, you will say, "Good work Aseem!" This call is only to calm my mind and focus on my work, sir.'

Chu studied Aseem for a long moment. Finally, he pushed his phone towards Aseem. 'One call. On speaker.'

Aseem's heart raced as he punched in the number of his own phone that he had given to Atul at the airport. The phone rang once, twice, before Atul's voice filled the room.

'Bhaiya, have you boarded the flight?'

'Aseem? Where are you? Are you okay?'

'I am great. Where are you?'

There was a pause on the other end before Atul spoke again. 'I couldn't just go and leave you here. I went to the Indian embassy. We will get you out.'

Chu's face contorted with rage. He slammed his fist on the desk, causing Aseem to flinch.

Aseem swallowed hard, his mind working frantically. 'Bhaiya, listen. You go home. Now. I am good here. This is good for me to make money. You know I want to make money.'

'But Aseem—'

'Bhaiya, you know I want money. You go home to ma and papa. They need you there. I want to be here.'

Chu snatched the phone away, ending the call abruptly. His eyes bore into Aseem, filled with suspicion.

'You think you're clever, don't you?' Chu spat. 'Your brother at the embassy . . .' He looked at Kovac and jerked his chin. Kovac took a step forward and moved his hand to grab Aseem's neck. But Aseem ducked and kept moving from one side of the room to the other, avoiding the burly man and talking all the while.

'Mr Chu, I had no idea . . . *Maa Kasam* . . . I swear on my mother's name . . . I told him to leave, you heard na. Please, give me one chance.'

Chu seemed to be enjoying how Aseem kept avoiding Kovac's reach.

'I have good skills for your work . . . and I gave you a good deal too . . . person for person, same to same. No, I am better than Atul . . . he was useless to you . . . and you got money also . . . no? I will free Sharma . . .' Aseem would have kept talking but Kovac finally got to him. Grabbing his neck in his huge palm, he raised Aseem in the air with one hand.

Aseem started to choke, his hands and legs thrashing helplessly. Chu kept looking. Then his lips curled open just a little bit. 'One week. Show me how good you are. Any game and you will wish you had never set foot here.'

Kovac put him back down on the floor. Aseem nodded. He had bought himself some time, but Atul had complicated the situation. He needed to have a plan quickly—one that would keep him alive and get Atul safely home. But before all that he had to be convincing in his show of loyalty and usefulness to Chu and the compound.

As he was led back to the workers' quarters, Aseem began to make a mental note of everything he saw. He had to catalogue everything about the compound, its routines and the people within it, while appearing to be nothing more than an eager new recruit.

The game was on and Aseem was playing for the highest stakes of his life.

3

Atul sat on the edge of the narrow bed in his small, functional hotel room. The room was sparsely furnished with just the essentials—a bed, a lamp, a fan and a wooden chair—but it was clean. The single window opened onto a busy street where Atul had stopped for food before stepping inside. A proper meal after so long had made him overeat. He could barely keep his eyes open now but he had to do one thing before crashing on the bed.

He took a deep breath, trying to steady his nerves, and dialled his home number. The phone rang a few times before his father picked up.

'Hello?' Anand's voice sounded tired.

'Papa . . .' Atul choked, and his voice broke off.

'Atul! Is that you, beta?'

'Yes, it's me, papa.'

'Are you alright? Where are you?' Anand's voice was a mix of surprise and relief.

'I'm free . . . I'm fine, papa,' Atul reassured him. 'Is everyone at home okay?'

'We were worried about you. But now everything will be fine. Only Aseem . . . Aseem is not here.' Anand completed the sentence somehow, not wanting to talk about his other son right then. Tulsi had come up to stand next to him. Radhika and Tulika had also emerged from their room.

'I need to tell you something about Aseem.'

'Did Aseem give them money to free you?' Anand tried to connect dots as he recovered from the surprise. 'When are you coming?'

'Aseem . . . he came here . . . to get me out,' Atul said, struggling to find the right words.

'There . . . Aseem?' Anand reacted in disbelief. His eyes moved from person to person around him.

'Aseem took my place . . . so I could come home. He did that for me, papa.'

There was a long pause on the other end of the line.

'Aseem took your place? Meaning he is . . .' Anand asked with a trembling voice. He wanted to know more but his voice failed.

'I will not leave him here,' Atul said, tears streaming down his face. 'I will bring him home.'

After a few more words that he didn't even remember later, Atul ended the call. He lay down, hoping sleep would come easily, but he kept thinking about his brother for a long time that night.

4

The ceiling fan's rhythmic creaking was the only sound breaking the silence. The phone was still clutched in Anand's right fist. He looked at his family—Tulsi on the floor cushion, a *jaapmala* frozen in her hands; Radhika perched on the chair's edge; and Tulika, who kept glancing at him. They had heard enough to be first relieved and then confused.

'Atul is free,' Anand finally spoke. He swallowed hard before continuing in a strangled voice. 'He's trying to get Aseem out. Aseem exchanged himself for Atul.'

The jaapmala snapped, scattering the prayer beads across the floor. Nobody moved to pick them up.

Radhika pressed her palms against her eyes. 'All this time he was doing that . . . while I was here judging him . . .'

Tulsi reached for the nearest bead, but her hand trembled too much to grasp it.

Tulika slid down to the floor, gathering the beads one by one. 'That's why he didn't explain. He couldn't.' She looked up at her father. 'What do we do now?'

Anand placed the phone on the table with deliberate care, as if it might shatter. 'We wait.' His jaw clenched. 'And this time, we trust him.'

5

In the days that followed, Aseem threw himself into his new role with the excitement of a child who has been given a new toy. He devoured the training manual and created fake profiles with a creativity that surprised even the seasoned team leaders. He seemed to enjoy it. Chu had seen a few such characters in his time, people who were driven by the greed of a good life over everything else.

'Man, I was born for this!' Aseem exclaimed, slapping his hand on the desk after luring a man registered on a dating site to sign in for their exclusive (fake) club. The supervisor nearby raised an eyebrow, amused by the newcomer's apparent zeal.

As he participated in the scams alongside more experienced captive workers, Aseem kept his ears open and his mouth running. 'Wish I had found this opportunity earlier,' he would say, loud enough for the manager to overhear. 'I could've been living the high life by now!'

Aseem's natural charm proved helpful as he moved around, armed with his silly jokes. 'This guy in my gym once told me he broke his arm in two places. I told him to stop going to those places!' and 'Why don't certain couples go to the gym? Because some relationships just don't work out!' He would keep repeating them whenever he saw a new person. He didn't mind if the individual ignored him or if a guard scowled—his smile, which only he knew was a facade, stayed fixed on his face all day every day. Gradually, some people began to warm to him, succumbing to his persistent cheerfulness. Some even started requesting him for a joke, and sometimes, asked him to repeat one for their friends.

Vikas and Sudhakar watched Aseem going about with his antics from across the work floor and their faces tightened with disapproval. They remembered Atul's quiet dignity, his refusal to participate in the scams despite the torture. Now here was his brother, laughing, joking and enjoying the same thing.

'Look at him, acting like this is some college fest.' Vikas's fingers struck the keyboard harder. 'I will slap him one day.'

'Can't believe he is Atul's brother,' Sudhakar added.

'I would not have believed it either if he had not been going around saying Atul couldn't do these scams even if he wanted to,' Vikas said in a hushed, angry voice. 'He is so annoying.'

Later that day, during lunch, Aseem sat down next to them uninvited. 'Hey guys, want to hear a joke . . .'

'We're not interested,' Vikas cut him off.

'How are you not ashamed of yourself? After what they did to your brother?' Sudhakar asked, not trying to hide his dislike.

Aseem's perpetual grin didn't waver. He leaned in, pretending to reach for the salt, and said softly, 'Wait and watch what I do to them.'

Over the next few days, they spoke in snippets whenever they were alone and away from the camera.

'I traded places with Atul. I got him out. You think I came here for fun?' Aseem told them.

Vikas's eyes widened. 'You got Atul out?'

'We were worried that something bad had happened. He disappeared so suddenly,' Sudhakar added.

'I can get us out too. But only if they think I love it here and I'm one of them,' Aseem assured them.

They developed a system. Vikas and Sudhakar would openly snub Aseem but secretly pass on any information they were able to get. They were looking for a gap in security, a way to escape.

Then the day came when Aseem got to attend his first party. Sudhakar and Vikas had briefed him about the parties. These were held once every two weeks to reward the achievers, those who had met their targets. They warned him that these parties were also a mechanism to get the workers to spend more, keeping them in a never-ending cycle of debt.

It took place in a large hall in the second building inside the compound. This building resembled a warehouse. The ambience was boisterous and indulgent. Loud music blared in the background. Alcohol and drugs were in abundance and the barrier between workers and guards had diminished in this setting. Aseem observed that the guards had also lowered their inhibitions for the first time and were fooling around. One of them even asked Aseem to tell a joke.

He played his part, laughing and joking, a drink in his hand. He even danced with some of the women who were clearly there to entertain and entice the workers. There were women co-workers, but these came from outside just for the party. Aseem wondered if they could be his way outside. He took in every detail of his surroundings. As the night progressed, the party became wilder and more debauched. Aseem saw an opportunity in the chaos and made his way towards the back of the room where he had noticed a door. He wanted to see what was behind it. He waited for the right moment— he had the age-old excuse of looking for the bathroom ready in case a guard questioned him. But he didn't need it. A fight broke out, attracting the attention of everyone in the room. He used the opportunity to slip away.

The door led him to what looked like a storage room. He saw a set of shelves loaded with cleaning supplies and maintenance equipment. Aseem's mind immediately began assessing the potential usefulness of some of the things kept there. He could use the strong toilet cleaners to corrode the barred windows in their living quarters. Or start a fire. But then what? In any case, the bottle was too big to carry through the party unnoticed, even if everyone was drunk. He parked the idea as a mental note for the time being.

He didn't know how he would escape eventually, but he mulled over any option that came to his mind—in the supply truck, with the girls who came for the parties, jumping over the wall, digging a way out below the wall or faking some health issue that would make them take him to a hospital—but he could see potential pitfalls in each of those plans. He could not risk a failed attempt because he may not get a second chance. All through this, he kept telling himself that he would find a way out.

He returned to the hall. The fight seemed to have died down and the party was back to normal, even more wild if anything. He decided to find Vikas and Sudhakar, but something struck his foot. Looking down, he struggled to see what it was due to the strobing lights and just picked it up. A mobile phone, possibly belonging to one of the guards or one of the girls who came from outside. He looked around, checking if anyone had noticed. He tapped the phone and the screen light came on. However, it prompted for a face ID or passcode to unlock it. Aseem's thrill changed into dismay. What rotten luck! He turned to leave, only to find Kovac staring at him.

'I . . . I was going to hand it to the guards . . . someone must have dropped it,' Aseem attempted to clarify. Kovac's suspicious gaze remained unchanged. Aseem doubted whether the hulking man even registered his words. The booming music made communication nearly impossible. Kovac seized him by the neck and pulled him to a remote corner.

'What were you doing with that phone?' he demanded.

Aseem quickly gave it to him. 'It's not mine . . . I found it on the floor. I was coming to hand it over.'

Kovac examined the phone and saw it was locked. That seemed to satisfy him. Yet, he wasn't done. His grip on Aseem's neck tightened. 'You shouldn't have picked it up. Don't think I trust you . . . I trust no one. Consider this a warning. The next time I catch you doing something shady, you'll regret it!' Kovac warned him. Aseem nodded, or as much as he could with his neck pinned in that huge hand. Kovac finally released his grip. Aseem thanked him profusely while rubbing his neck.

Aseem walked across the hall, intending to head back to his room. *Enough excitement for one night, better to have a good sleep now.* But as fate would have it, the night had other plans. While passing the makeshift bar area, his attention was caught by the bartender's action—he was plugging his phone into a charger at the corner of the counter.

Time seemed to slow down as an idea formed in Aseem's mind. He approached the bar, trying hard to sound casual, and leaned against the counter. 'Can I get an LIIT?' he asked, choosing the cocktail he knew with the most number of ingredients. The bartender nodded and turned away, focused on making the drink.

The phone lay there, unguarded, its screen still glowing. Aseem's hand moved almost of its own accord, fingers closing around the device. He stepped away and crouched down in a shadowed corner behind the bar, his back pressed against the wall.

The phone's screen remained mercifully unlocked. Aseem's hands trembled as he held it, his heart thundering so loud he was sure others could hear it. With every passing second, he expected to feel Kovac's iron grip on his neck again. Despite his fear, his fingers moved across the screen.

6

Atul had recounted every detail he could remember about the compound and the people there to Avinash and his team. The layout, the guards, the manager, the names that he knew, the daily routines—Atul had shared it all, hoping it would somehow be enough to locate and rescue his brother.

He had taken details of the case filed in Delhi and shared those too. He knew that Kapoor and DCP Singh had spoken with each other, and though the DCP was not at all happy with what Aseem had done, he had promised to continue pursuing the case at his end and would arrange to bring back the brothers and anyone else Kapoor was able to rescue.

The embassy officials collaborated with local Cambodian police, using Atul's information to narrow down potential locations. From the driving time and other descriptions Atul had provided, they had concluded that this particular compound must be in Kampong Speu province. That was the easy part, Avinash told Atul—the difficult part was that the area had seen a rapid proliferation of scam compounds in more rural areas and they were often harder to detect due to their remote locations.

The police investigation, aided by local intelligence, had come up with multiple potential sites. However, conducting a raid on one would risk alerting others. And there was no guarantee that a potential compound was actually running some illicit operation.

Kapoor was determined to pinpoint the location though, not only for Aseem, but also because approximately a hundred Indians were being held captive there. Rescuing all of them was of great significance to the embassy. They were aware that various scam compounds housed workers from different nationalities. Reports indicated that individuals from China, Malaysia, Indonesia and Vietnam had been coerced into similar scamming activities targeting their own countrymen. Kapoor had requested DCP Gurnam Singh to obtain satellite imagery of the area. Yet, the process was taking longer than anticipated, adding to everyone's frustration. But none more than Atul.

After one more day of frustration, he lay on his hotel bed, his mind in turmoil. Kapoor was kind and helpful, but Atul wished he could move to rescue Aseem before it was too late. He was unable to sleep but it turned out to be a good thing, because when a message pinged from an unknown number, he saw it immediately.

7

Radhika stared at the blueprint spread across her desk but her mind kept drifting to Aseem. Everything she had believed about her younger brother had turned upside down in the last few days. The brother whom she thought could not see beyond himself had sacrificed his freedom for Atul. The irony was bitter—if she had known Aseem's true intentions, would she have accepted Jayesh's proposal so readily? Back then, with both brothers seemingly lost forever and her father's life savings—including her marriage fund—gone, she had convinced herself she was stepping up for the family. But there was something else too driving her decision. After all, if Jayesh could manipulate her feelings for personal interest, and if

Aseem could betray his family so completely for his own gain (or so she had thought), then why should she play by different rules?

'Earth to Radhika?' Jayesh's voice broke through her thoughts. He stood in her office doorway, two coffee cups in hand. Their first meeting since announcing their decision to their families. 'Thought you might need this.'

She accepted the coffee, noting how he had remembered her preference for extra sugar. The small gestures of friendship were slowly returning, making their workplace interactions less awkward. 'Thanks. I needed to discuss the Noida project with you anyway. The contractors are pushing back on the timeline.'

'And you could not terrify them into submission?' he asked in a mock surprise.

'I use that selectively,' she said, then added more seriously, 'Though I could use your help. Some of these guys are your father's buddies.'

Jayesh's smile faded slightly at the mention of his father. 'Speaking of fathers . . . how's yours taking the news?'

Radhika couldn't help but laugh. 'You mean besides asking for the fifth time if your parents have given us their blessings?'

'He cares for you.' Jayesh chuckled. 'Mine is just relieved I'm marrying a girl. But I think he is a bit worried about "the girl from Mandawali".' He paused, fidgeting with his coffee cup. 'Have you given a thought to moving your parents to a better house?'

Radhika's eyes narrowed. 'Are you trying to package us better?'

'No . . . I just think it will be good for them. A three-bedroom apartment in a society in Patparganj?'

'We can't accept—'

'I am not offering. You are earning enough now. Though I am open to giving you a loan.'

'Loan your ass, Jayesh Gupta . . . half of everything you own will be mine after marriage. Have you thought about that?'

'Hey, don't bring in my ass . . . I am very touchy about it,' Jayesh said with a dramatic seriousness that made Radhika laugh.

'Okay . . . I will start looking,' she said.

'Cool . . . now that that is settled, would you like to go out for dinner tonight? We should be seen together more often.'

'I can't.' Radhika's smile faded. Jayesh was being selfish and not caring about her feelings, but she didn't make it obvious. 'With all the uncertainties about Aseem and Atul . . . I have to be with my family.'

'Hey,' Jayesh reached across the desk, then seemed to think better of it. 'Should we delay the engagement? With everything your family's going through—'

'No,' Radhika straightened. 'This actually helps. Gives them something to focus on besides worrying. And Tulika is making biryani.'

'What?' Jayesh was confused by the sudden change of topic.

'Tulika is making biryani. That is one more reason I can't go out with you.'

'I could come over?' he said. The offer surprised Radhika. 'I mean, I should spend more time with your family anyway.'

'Listen, Mr US returnee Defence Colony brat, do not kill yourself while trying to impress. You will not survive ten minutes in Mandawali.'

'You want to bet, Ms Mandawali?'

Her phone buzzed—a message from Tulika: 'You want to bring your boyfriend home? I made extra biryani.'

Radhika looked at Jayesh. *He was a good boy, even if complicated.* She smiled despite herself. He was her gateway to be someone. He was her chance to a better life. And, she liked being with him. She realized in that moment that she would have accepted his offer even if she knew Aseem's real plan. Not knowing had just made it easier.

8

Atul burst out of his hotel and ran towards the embassy. He made it halfway down the street before common sense caught up with him. The embassy would be closed at this hour—and he had Avinash's number.

His fingers trembled as he dialled. 'Sir . . . Aseem . . . he sent a location!' The words tumbled out as soon as Kapoor's sleepy voice answered.

'Stay at the hotel. I will come and get you.' Sleep vanished from Kapoor's voice.

The next forty minutes moved very slowly as Atul waited outside the hotel. His mind doing every possible permutation of the things that could have gone wrong—from him mishearing what Avinash had said to a car accident that sent him to hospital to him going back to sleep after his call. The spiralling only ceased when a convoy of vehicles—three police cars, one embassy SUV and an ambulance—stopped in front of the modest hotel. 'Get in quickly.' said Kapoor, opening the door for Atul. It was clear he had mobilized a raid party and really fast. 'You are with me. Remember—stay back when we enter.'

Atul sat in the back of Kapoor's vehicle, his heart hammering against his ribs. The streets of Phnom Penh gave way to darker, rural roads.

'Five minutes out,' a voice on a radio announced.

Atul's hands clenched into fists. The last time he was going this way, he had been so hopeful and full of dreams. Now he was terrified. He prayed fervently. 'Let Aseem come out of this safe, Durga Ma . . . help us, Baba Baidyanath.' He kept praying to all the gods he could think of as their destination got closer.

A familiar compound emerged from the darkness—concrete walls topped with barbed wire, cutting a harsh silhouette against the star-studded sky. The front gate stood partially open, the guard post empty.

'Something's wrong,' Atul muttered.

Teams moved in with practiced precision but met no resistance.

They moved through the building systematically. All the doors were ajar. In the work area, computers were still on desks, but the chairs were empty.

Room after room told the same story. Signs of hasty departure were present everywhere. Atul recognized the dormitory where he had slept, the beds still unmade. The raid party's footsteps echoed in the eerie silence.

The calls echoed through the building as room after room was declared clear by the raid party, each one driving the knife deeper into Atul's gut.

Kapoor's face was like stone as the local police chief approached. 'They knew we were coming,' the chief said, his accent thick with frustration. 'We found eight people in all. Aseem is not one of them.'

'A leak,' Kapoor's voice was cold. 'Someone tipped them off.'

Atul slumped against a wall, sliding down until he sat on the floor. 'Aseem,' he whispered. 'He risked everything to send that location. If they caught him . . .' He couldn't finish the thought.

Kapoor sat beside him. 'This isn't over. Aseem found a way to contact us once—that shows he's smart. He'll find another way.'

But Atul barely heard him. All he could think about was *What if he got exposed?* 'Please,' he whispered. 'Please stay alive.'

9

The bus lurched through the darkness, its engine growling against the reigning silence. Inside, the sickly-sweet smell of alcohol hung heavy in the air. Around him, his fellow captives swayed in their seats, most of them in deep sleep. The few who were still awake wore expressions of confused fear.

Aseem's mind went back to the events that had transpired. Though he went to his room after sending the location to Atul, every minute felt like a ticking time bomb. He kept expecting to be dragged out for questioning. When chaos erupted and they were herded into the open compound, Aseem knew they had discovered something. They were all put into two buses. The compound's sudden evacuation confirmed his fears, but at least his cover hadn't been blown.

Now, as the bus crawled through the jungle on a dirt track barely wide enough for it, Aseem's racing thoughts crystallized into determination. They were avoiding the main roads, he realized. *The police must be looking for us. It's now or never.*

Kovac sat four rows ahead, his massive frame a dark silhouette against the windshield. Five guards were spread across the front seats, fighting to stay awake. There was a bus ahead of them under Chu's watch. Beside Aseem, Vikas's head lolled against the window, while Sudhakar's soft snores came from across the aisle.

Aseem's fingers trembled slightly as he shook them both. 'Stay awake,' he whispered, his voice barely audible above the engine's rumble. Before they could fully register his words, he stood up, channelling every ounce of courage he could muster.

'Hello, sleeping beauties!' His voice cracked slightly, but he pushed through. 'The party's not over yet!' The words echoed in the silent bus, making several captives flinch. Aseem started humming, his voice growing stronger with each note. '*Subah hone na den . . . Saath khone na den . . .* Let's play antakshari . . . *Main tera hero . . .*'

A guard turned, his face twisted in annoyance. 'Shut up and sit—'

But another voice joined in, trembling at first, then stronger. Then another. The hit tune spread through the bus like a wave. The night's revelries meant that the fear levels were considerably low.

A young guard in the middle even started tapping his foot, caught up in the moment.

Aseem swayed down the aisle, in calculated drunken stumble. His mind flashed back to the countless beatings he had witnessed in the compound. *One chance. That's all I've got.*

'Got any songs for us, big guy?' he slurred, reaching Kovac's row. The security chief's eyes narrowed dangerously, reminding Aseem of a cobra about to strike.

'Back. To. Your. Seat.' Each word carried a promise of violence.

Aseem raised his hands in mock surrender and turned, quickly surveying each guard. The one in the second row was nodding off, his stun gun loose in his holster. *Perfect.*

'Alright, party pooper, I'll just—' He lunged, fingers closing around the stun gun's grip. The guard's eyes widened in delayed recognition as Aseem pressed the gun against his neck and pulled the trigger.

The guard convulsed, but Aseem had no time to watch him fall. Kovac sprang out from his seat with more agility than Aseem could have expected. Aseem tried to use the stun gun on him, but the big hands wrapped around his throat and lifted him. Kovac's face filled his vision, teeth bared in a snarl. Kovac's right hand squeezed Aseem's neck with crushing force while his left hand tried to take the stun gun. Aseem refused to let go. Just as it seemed he was going to lose, one girl from the captives lunged at them. Kovac swatted her away like a fly with his left hand, but it gave Aseem the opportunity to press the gun against his neck. Aseem pressed the trigger and held it there, even as Kovac squeezed his neck as tightly as he could. Black spots danced at the edges of Aseem's vision as he felt faint. Finally Kovac's grip loosened. Using the last of his strength, Aseem pushed, sending the massive man crashing to the floor.

The bus skidded to a stop. The driver opened the door on his side, jumped out and ran away. Through the windshield, Aseem could see the taillights of the second bus disappearing around a bend. *Chu hasn't noticed yet. But for how long?*

'Everyone out!' Aseem screamed, yanking the door open. 'Into the jungle! Now!'

They poured out into the darkness, adrenaline overriding fear. They tried to take everyone along, but some were just too high and beyond walking. The moon cast strange shadows through the foliage of looming trees as the captives ran beneath it. Some stumbled, others ran with surprising speed. Behind them, Kovac's roar of rage echoed through the jungle, followed by the sound of pursuit.

Aseem's lungs burned as he ran, branches whipping his face. The darkness was almost complete, save for occasional shafts of moonlight piercing the canopy. He counted small victories: no firearms spotted on the guards, the element of surprise, the distance they had gained . . .

A gunshot shattered his optimism.

Wood splintered somewhere nearby and Aseem dove behind a tree. All around him, people scattered like startled birds, dropping to the ground or pressing themselves against trees. The jungle fell silent except for heavy breathing and distant shouts.

He caught movement in his peripheral vision and turned—too late. A body slammed into him, sending them both rolling down a slope. Hands clawed at his throat. In desperation, Aseem's fingers found a rock. He swung without thinking, connecting with a thud. The guard went limp and Aseem scrambled to his feet, his chest heaving. A familiar shadow approached him.

'There are only twelve or thirteen of them,' Vikas's voice came from the darkness, trembling but determined. 'We outnumber them. We should fight.'

'They have guns—' Aseem started to respond but stopped as Maya stepped forward and took the stone from his hand. She swooped down and smashed it on the head of the fallen guard. The crack of bone and a muffled scream split the night.

'Let's reduce their numbers whenever we can.' Maya whispered, her voice breaking. In the dim light, Aseem saw tears streaming down her face. 'I can't go back there. I won't.'

Aseem did not know Maya as well as he knew Vikas and Sudhakar, but he recognized her as the only person with courage to attack Kovac in the bus, giving him the chance to use the stun gun. The place had broken something in all of them, Aseem realized. Or maybe it had forged something new—something harder.

'We won't go back,' Aseem promised. He quickly counted the shadows gathering around them—sixteen people. Not everyone had made it this far, but it would have to be enough.

'Grab anything you can use as a weapon,' he ordered softly, trying to project confidence he himself was trying to muster. 'Stay close. Stay quiet.' He looked back toward the sounds of pursuit. The night was far from over.

10

The sounds had grown fainter. Aseem's steps slowed, hope flickering in his chest for the first time since they had fled. The others collected around him, stumbling rather than moving, their breaths coming in ragged gasps.

Then he heard it. A scream. Far off to their right, but clear enough to stop everyone in their tracks. Shouts followed. It sounded like the guards and came from somewhere behind them. The hope was replaced by a cold understanding—the sound of pursuit had grown faint because the hunters had split up.

'Quiet,' he whispered, raising his hand. The group huddled closer, their earlier relief curdling into fear. More screams echoed through the trees. Whoever had been caught was putting up a fight.

Aseem's mind raced. They were being hunted from two directions. Some of their fellow escapees had been caught. And they were next.

What would Chu be thinking right now? The image of the thin manager came to mind, his menacing cold eyes. He would be expecting them to run, to keep running until they were too exhausted to fight back.

'We need to move,' someone whispered urgently.

'No.' Aseem surprised himself with the firmness in his voice. He looked around at the dark shapes of trees surrounding them. 'We wait here.'

'Wait? Are you crazy?'

Maybe he was. But running blindly had only split them up and made them easier targets. 'They think we're desperate, running scared.' His voice grew stronger as the plan took shape. 'Let's give them a surprise instead.'

He didn't have time to second-guess himself. The sounds were getting closer—footsteps, branches snapping. Quickly, he directed people to collect as many rocks as they could, then take cover or climb up the trees. He himself picked up a rock and slid behind a thick trunk.

The first figure that emerged from the darkness was one of Chu's men, moving cautiously. Then another. Chu himself appeared, moonlight glinting off of his pistol.

Aseem threw the first rock. It whizzed past Chu's head, making him spin around and fire blindly into the darkness. Another rock came and hit a guard on his head. Then another and soon there was a barrage of them. The first guard went down, clutching his head. Another stumbled back as a rock caught him in the chest. Chu fired again and again, but in the chaos his shots went wild, exploding harmlessly into tree trunks.

'Find them!' Chu's voice cracked with rage. 'They're just—' A rock caught him in the shoulder, spinning him around.

The former captives jumped down from the trees, others came out from hiding, the hunters turned into the hunted in the face of this ambush. Chu had run out of bullets and screamed at his men to retreat.

As their footsteps faded, Aseem sagged against a tree, his legs weak with relief. But there was no time to celebrate. The night had grown colder, or maybe it was just fear settling into his bones. They had won a skirmish, but Kovac . . . Kovac was different.

Vikas limped closer to him. 'What do we do now?'

Before Aseem could answer, a roar shattered the night's silence. It wasn't the sound of anger—it was worse. It was the sound of someone enjoying the hunt. The leaves trembled with heavy footfalls approaching their position.

'Spread out,' Aseem whispered, his mouth dry. 'Don't bunch together.' The words felt inadequate. What strategy could work against a man who enjoyed violence?

They emerged from the darkness like a nightmare. Kovac in the lead, his massive frame somehow larger in the moonlight, followed by guards dragging their captured companions. The security chief's knuckles were already bloodied.

For a moment, both groups stood frozen, sizing each other up. Aseem saw the defeat in the eyes of the captured escapees, saw how some couldn't even stand straight. His earlier encounters with Kovac flashed through his mind—the raw power, the casual brutality.

'The hero returns,' Kovac's voice carried a hint of amusement. 'Did you really think you could get away from me?' He stepped forward, moonlight catching the cruel smile on his face. 'Look around you. Look what happened to your friends who tried to fight.'

Aseem wanted to run. Every instinct screamed at him to flee. But he knew that running was exactly what Kovac wanted. The giant wanted to hunt, to break them one by one.

'It's over,' Kovac continued, taking another step. 'Surrender now and I might even let you keep some of your teeth.'

Something snapped inside Aseem. Maybe it was fear transforming into desperate courage, or maybe it was just the absurdity of it all—him, a small-time gym trainer, facing this monster.

'You know what, Kovac?' His voice shook, but he forced out a laugh. 'Want to hear a joke?'

The giant's eyes narrowed, caught off guard by this unexpected response.

'You're really brave in the compound, aren't you? Breaking people who can't fight back?' Aseem's words came faster now, fuelled by fear and rage. 'But out here? Out here, you, *you* are the joke. A bully who's about to learn—'

He didn't get to finish. Kovac moved with frightening speed. His swing could have taken Aseem's head off if panic hadn't made him stumble backwards. The displacement of air alone made his skin prickle.

'I'll show you who is the joke,' Kovac snarled, advancing like an avalanche. 'I'll show you what happens to little men who talk too much.'

'Fight me big mouth,' Kovac further taunted. 'Teach me a lesson.'

Aseem scrambled to keep his distance, his mind racing. He had spent a lot of time watching people move, correcting their form, understanding how bodies worked. But this was different. This was survival.

Another punch came, closer this time. Aseem could smell the metallic scent of blood on Kovac's knuckles as they whistled past his nose.

'Stop dancing!' Kovac lunged forward and his fist connected. The impact against Aseem's side felt like being hit by a truck. He sprawled into the dirt, his mouth filling with the taste of earth. His ribs hurt like hell as he tried to roll away.

Kovac's shadow fell over him. 'I'm going to make you regret every second of this,' the giant growled, reaching down.

Time seemed to slow. Aseem saw the massive hand descending, remembered how it had crushed throats before. His fingers dug into the ground beside him, seeking purchase to push himself up. Instead, they sank into soft earth.

Mud.

Without thinking, Aseem grabbed a handful and threw it upward just as Kovac's face came close. The dirt splattered across the giant's eyes. The roar that followed was deafening, more animal than human.

'YOU . . .' Kovac staggered back, pawing at his eyes. His next words were lost in rage.

'NOW!' Aseem screamed. He hadn't planned this, hadn't coordinated anything, but something in his voice, in this moment of the giant's vulnerability, sparked action.

They came from all directions, both his group and the recently captured others. They grabbed at Kovac's limbs, clinging like desperate survivors in a storm. Some of them turned to the other guards, fighting with a courage born out of sheer desperation. The giant thrashed, still half-blinded, his fists connecting with terrible impact whenever they found a target.

Bodies went flying. Someone's nose burst in a spray of blood. But for every person Kovac threw off, two more latched on. Their weight began to affect even his incredible strength. He stumbled, trying to shake them loose.

Aseem watched, his side burning with each breath, searching for an opening. This was their only chance. If Kovac recovered . . .

Then he saw a chance. The giant's movements were becoming wilder, less controlled. His head whipped back and forth, trying to track threats he couldn't see clearly. Aseem forced himself to his feet, ignoring the protest from his ribs.

'Keep holding him!' he shouted, then ran forward. Using the backs and shoulders of others as stepping stones, he scrambled up the human pile and jumped. His legs locked around Kovac's neck as his hands found a hold on the giant's head.

What happened next was pure instinct. No technique, no finesse—just desperate strength and the will to survive. Aseem twisted with everything he had, feeling muscles strain and tendons pop beneath his grip.

For a moment that stretched into eternity, nothing happened. Then, like an ancient tree finally yielding to a raging storm, Kovac began to fall. The impact shook the earth as the giant's massive frame finally went still.

For several heartbeats, no one moved. The only sounds were ragged breathing and the rustling of leaves. Aseem rolled off Kovac's unconscious form, every muscle on fire. His hands were shaking so badly he could barely push himself up.

'Is he . . .' someone whispered.

'Still breathing,' Aseem managed, watching the rise and fall of the giant's chest. Part of him wanted to make sure Kovac would never get up again, never hurt anyone else. But that wasn't who he was.

'Quick,' he gasped, 'bind him.'

They worked fast, using vines to secure Kovac to a thick tree. Some of the guards had been beaten and overpowered. The remaining had melted into the jungle during the fight, probably running back to find Chu.

Aseem looked at the faces around him—bruised and bloody, but alive. All wore the same expression: a surreal mixture of disbelief and hope.

'Anyone who can't walk?' he asked, forcing himself to focus. A few raised their hands. Others stepped forward to support them.

'The road,' one woman said. 'I heard trucks earlier. Must be close.'

Aseem nodded, trying to ignore the throbbing in his side. 'We move together,' he said. 'No one gets left behind. Not now.'

They started walking, helping those who stumbled. The jungle seemed different now, less threatening, or maybe they were just too exhausted to feel fear. The first hints of dawn were beginning to lighten the sky, turning black shadows to grey.

When they finally broke through the treeline onto a dirt road, the sun was just peeking over the horizon. They stood there, blinking in the growing light, hardly daring to believe it was real.

Someone started crying. Then another. Soon half the group was in tears, not from sadness, but from something deeper. Relief. Exhaustion. Freedom.

Aseem watched them, his own eyes burning. Back home, he was the one with big plans that never worked out. Now he had led these people to freedom. The thought felt too immense to process.

'Thank you,' someone said, touching his arm. Others joined in, reaching out to clasp his hand, pat his shoulder.

A sound in the distance made them all tense—but it was just a truck, an ordinary delivery vehicle approaching on the road.

'Come on,' he said, stepping onto the road as the truck went past them. 'Let's go home.'

11

The morning sun beat down on Aseem's shoulders as he staggered forward, each step sending fresh waves of pain through his bruised ribs. Behind him, the ragged line of escapees stretched out along the dusty road, their shadows long in the early light.

'Look!' someone's hoarse cry broke the rhythm of shuffling feet. 'A bus station!'

Through the heat haze, a small depot materialized, its faded blue sign creaking in the breeze. Aseem squinted at the Khmer script, the unfamiliar characters swimming before his eyes. The few parked buses and waiting passengers told them what the unfamiliar language could not. His knees nearly buckled as he lowered himself onto a wooden bench, the splintered slats digging into his thighs.

'We did it,' whispered Maya as she slumped beside him, dried blood still crusting her temple. 'We actually made it.'

Around them, others collapsed onto benches or simply sat on the ground, their faces marked with exhaustion and something else—hope, or at least its tender beginning. A few of the stronger ones moved toward the ticket counter, pooling together the money that was still left from the party.

Aseem's throat felt like sandpaper. He needed to call Atul, needed to let him know . . . His eyes scanned the station for a public phone, finding nothing but curious stares from the locals. An elderly woman sat nearby, a smartphone visible in her hand.

'Excuse me,' he croaked, approaching her with what he hoped was a non-threatening smile. He mimicked making a phone call. 'Please? Just one call?'

The woman's eyes widened as she took in his appearance—torn clothes, mud-caked hair, the bruises. She clutched her bag closer, shaking her head rapidly. Two more attempts with other passengers yielded similar results.

'Aseem!' the urgency in Vikas's voice made him turn. A police officer was approaching. The man barked something in Khmer, his hand casually resting on his holster.

More officers appeared, surrounding their group. One stepped forward, his English broken but his authority clear: 'Papers. Passports?'

Aseem's stomach clenched. He glanced at his companions—all bearing visible signs of their fight for freedom, some still bleeding. How could he explain what they had been through? The words felt inadequate even in his head.

'Please,' he started, 'we were held captive. There's a compound in the jungle where they—'

'No papers?' The officer's face hardened. 'You come with us. Now.'

12

The processing room at the police station smelled of stale cigarettes and urine. One by one, they were photographed, fingerprinted, their names entered into a system that would mark them as criminals rather than survivors. Aseem's demands for a phone call echoed off of concrete walls, met only with blank stares or sharp commands in Khmer. *Why can't they understand what they have been through?*

The holding cell was crowded. A younger man—barely more than a boy really—pressed against the bars. 'What happens now?' His question carried the weight of all their fears.

'We escaped just to end up in another prison?' Vikas said, sounding desperate.

Aseem felt their eyes on him, searching for the leader that had gotten them through the night. He forced himself to stand straighter.

'Tomorrow, we start demanding to speak to the Indian embassy,' he said, trying to inject certainty into his voice. 'Every hour if we have to.' He met their gazes one by one. 'We're not criminals hiding from the law. We're survivors with a story to tell. And I promise you—someone's going to listen.'

Those words may not have been of much comfort to the worn-out souls in the cell, but it was something to hold on to. Aseem leaned against the wall, his exhausted mind already working on their next move. They had fought too hard, come too far, to let concrete walls and iron bars be the end of their story.

13

Atul couldn't sleep the night of the failed raid. The weight of thoughts was too strong. His mind raced with scenarios of what could have gone wrong, each more terrifying than the last. The thought he tried hardest to suppress kept surfacing—had Aseem paid a terrible price for sending that message?

His phone lay silent on the bedside table, its dark screen offering no answers. Every few minutes, he would pick it up, check for messages, then toss it aside in frustration. When exhaustion finally forced him to the bed, sleep still wouldn't come. The irony wasn't lost on him—he, the elder brother who was supposed to protect Aseem, now lay safe in a hotel room while his younger brother faced untold dangers.

The next day crawled by in the sterile halls of the embassy. Atul haunted Kapoor's office from morning till evening, desperate for news. Late afternoon brought grim updates: the police suspected the captives had been taken toward Koh Kong province near the Thailand border. Reports of gunfire in the forested area. Possible escape attempts. The police chief mentioned trafficking routes to Myanmar, where conditions were worse due to political instability.

'We haven't found any bodies,' Kapoor tried to reassure him, but Atul barely heard him. His world had narrowed to a single thought: he should have never let Aseem take his place.

Another sleepless night followed, the hotel room's silence broken only by his restless movements and racing thoughts.

On the third morning, just as he entered the embassy's marble-floored lobby, his phone rang. Unknown number.

'Hello?' His voice barely broke the silence.

'Bhai?' The familiar voice nearly brought him to his knees.

'Aseem!' Atul's hand trembled on the phone. 'Are you okay? Where are you?'

'I'm great.' Aseem's voice was tired but carried that familiar hint of confidence. 'Got quite a story to tell you, but right now I need help. We're at a police station.'

Aseem quickly explained their escape and current situation. 'Been trying to reach you for days. They finally let me use a phone.'

'Hold on,' Atul's voice strengthened with purpose. 'We'll get you out. Just . . . hold . . . stay on the line.'

He rushed to Kapoor's office, phone extended. After taking down the details, Avinash looked up with a rare smile. 'Your brother is a hero! He hasn't just saved himself, he has also rescued thirty others. And it started with you, Atul.'

Atul collapsed into the chair, tears flowing freely. All the fear, anxiety and guilt of the past few days poured out. Through his tears, he saw Kapoor quietly leave the room, giving him this moment of relief. His brother was alive.

Ten

1

THE AUTO'S TIRES CRUNCHED OVER loose gravel as Anand parked it in the narrow lane outside their home. His shoulders slumped with the weight of fifteen hours behind the wheel. The evening air, thick with Delhi's pollution, clung to his throat. He glanced at his watch. 7.45 p.m. Time for a quick dinner before his two-hour rest and another night shift. The interest payments wouldn't wait. Radhika had offered to help, but Anand had refused.

'First clear your office loan, beti,' he had said. He felt bad seeing her hurt expression. But principles were principles—how could he let his daughter carry his burden when she herself was in debt? Besides, this sudden rise in her fortune worried him. Three times the salary? A marriage proposal from the owner's son? In his simple world, such things didn't happen without a catch.

Inside their two-bedroom house, the rhythmic click-click of a jaapmala provided a constant backdrop to their evenings now. Tulsi sat cross-legged in her usual corner, her fingers moving mechanically over the beads while her lips formed silent prayers. The small altar beside her had grown—new pictures added along with more incense sticks. The scent of sandalwood filled the house.

'Chhoti, can you take out the food?' Tulsi called out without opening her eyes. She could tell from the footsteps that it was Anand. These days, she cooked half of what she used to. Yet, the steel containers in the kitchen held leftovers more often than not.

At her study table, Tulika was organizing her new books for UPSC mains prep, carefully stacking away the well-worn prelims material. The afternoon's conversation with Amit had left her feeling both lighter and more determined. They had spent hours analysing their prelims answers and his confidence in their performance was infectious. Then, in an unexpected moment, he had confessed his feelings, his voice trembling slightly. Her heart had skipped a beat—she felt the same way, but her dream of becoming an IPS officer had to come first. She told him that earlier she just wanted to clear the exam but now, after what her family had gone through, she resolved to get into the police service. His understanding smile when she explained this had only made her like him more. Now, looking at the fresh notebooks and unopened books for the mains, she felt a renewed sense of purpose. No time to waste waiting for results with two more stages to go.

The sounds of traffic and temple bells filtered through their thin walls as they sat down for dinner. There were only three plates on the small table—Radhika was out with Jayesh. Anand mechanically lifted rice to his mouth, his mind calculating loan instalments. Tulsi's eyes kept drifting to the empty chairs. The ceiling fan whirred overhead, ineffectually stirring the heavy air.

The sharp trill of a phone shattered the silence.

Anand's hand froze midway to his mouth, a few grains of rice falling unnoticed. Tulsi's fingers clutched the edge of the table. Tulika's breath caught in her throat as she watched her father's trembling hand reach for the phone.

In that moment before he answered, time seemed to stretch like a rubber band pulled taut, ready to either snap or spring back.

2

The doors to the big hall at the Indian embassy in Phnom Penh swung open. One by one, the exhausted group of escapees filed in, their faces reflecting both weariness and relief. Aseem entered last, making sure everyone was safely inside. His clothes were dirty and his face gaunt from days of hardship, but his eyes were already scanning the room, searching for one face.

Embassy staff moved quickly to attend to the group, offering water and directing them to chairs, but Aseem barely noticed. He had found who he was looking for.

'Bhai!' The word came out as a hoarse whisper.

The brothers collided in a fierce embrace, both trembling. Aseem could feel Atul's tears soaking into his already grimy shirt and realized he was crying too.

'God, Aseem,' Atul choked out, pulling back to examine his brother's bruised face and hollow cheeks. His eyes darted to the group being tended to by embassy staff. 'You actually did it. You got them all out.' Aseem didn't say anything.

Atul took another long look at his brother, trying to stop the tears. 'These past days . . . not knowing how you were after the compound raid had failed . . .'

'Oh, so that's why they moved us in such a hurry.' Aseem managed a weak smile. 'The compound wasn't too bad, but the escape and jail part got a bit scary.'

'Only you could say something like that!' Atul pulled him close again. 'You're insane, but you're the bravest person I know.'

Aseem shook his head against Atul's shoulder. 'I'm not brave. I was terrified the whole time. I just . . . didn't let anyone see it.'

Avinash Kapoor approached them, his expression warm. 'Take all the time you need, but Aseem should see the medical team soon. If all goes well with the paperwork, you both can fly home tomorrow.'

After thanking Avinash, Atul pulled out his phone. 'Let's call papa.'

'Do a video call,' Aseem told his brother.

It seemed like an eternity had passed before Anand's anxious face appeared on the screen, joined quickly by Tulsi and Tulika.

'Papa,' Atul and Aseem exclaimed together.

'Atul, Aseem!' Tulsi's voice cracked. 'Are you alright?'

'We're okay, ma,' Aseem assured her, noting how his mother had aged years in weeks. 'We're coming home tomorrow.'

'Son,' Anand's steady voice carried more emotion than Aseem had ever heard. 'We are so proud of you.'

A sudden scream of delight interrupted them as Radhika burst into the frame. 'Aseem . . . I'll kill you for tricking us like that, but first I'll hug you!'

Aseem managed a genuine laugh. 'It's okay, di. I had to maintain my reputation for crazy plans.'

After the call, the brothers sat in comfortable silence until a medical team arrived to check Aseem's injuries.

3

The next day at the airport, Aseem stared at the departure board, his injuries now properly dressed. 'Never thought I would be so happy looking at flight timings.'

Atul watched his brother's haunted expression. 'Aseem, what you did . . . sacrificing yourself for me . . .'

'Don't,' Aseem cut him off. 'I did what I had to do. Though . . .' A familiar mischievous glint returned to his eyes.

'Though what?'

Aseem turned to Atul with his trademark grin. 'You have to do something quickly to give me the money I need . . .'

Atul groaned. 'Already?'

'Hey, a deal's a deal. You're free because of me, remember?'

'And you'll never let me forget it, will you?'

'Not a chance, bhai. Not a chance.'

Both brothers laughed, heading home to their waiting family.

Epilogue

THE FARMHOUSE IN CHHATARPUR STOOD like a glittering palace, its driveway lined with clipped shrubs wrapped in twinkling lights. Crystal chandeliers cast a warm glow through the massive French windows of the white bungalow, while fountain jets danced to synchronized music. Fresh flowers cascaded from every archway and a band belted popular songs that nobody paid attention to. This was a celebration of their only son's thirtieth birthday and the Guptas had spared no expense in a bid to flaunt their prosperity. A surprise engagement ceremony was to follow, about which both Radhika and Jayesh's families, along with half of the guests, were already aware.

Near the buffet, Aseem was busy introducing Soni to every dish available, while Atul watched his younger brother with amused affection. Tulika noticed Radhika fidgeting with her phone and asked if everything was okay. Radhika squeezed her hand before slipping away to find Jayesh. She found him curled up on the bed in his reserved room.

'I can't breathe,' he gasped.

'Here,' she knelt beside him. 'Remember the breathing. Inhale slowly.'

After his breathing steadied, she tried one last time. 'Jayesh, you still have an option. Go away. Go where your heart is.'

'My father . . .' he started.

'Will eventually understand. Or maybe he won't. But you'll be free, living your truth.'

'I'll lose everything.'

'You're losing yourself right now and that's worse.'

'Hai Ram,' Tulsi whispered, clutching her silk saree. 'Look at those flowers! How much they must have spent just on decoration?'

Anand nodded, nervously adjusting his new kurta. Around them, fragments of conversation floated by, each a reminder of a world far removed from their own.

'My son's startup has investors lining up from Silicon Valley . . .'

'That's a Sabyasachi, but looks like last season darling . . .'

'We cancelled our Maldives holiday and went to Lakshadweep instead . . .'

Tulsi glanced at Anand with playful reproach. 'You never take me anywhere.'

'Didn't we visit Baba Dhaam?' Anand attempted to deflect.

'That was seven years ago.' Tulsi wasn't about to let him off easily.

'Alright... where would you like to go?' Anand relented.

'Banaras! I want to visit the Baba Vishwanath temple,' she declared and her husband agreed without hesitation.

'Done! Let's go next week.'

Tulsi's eyes sparkled with delight.

Half an hour later, the family regrouped in the main hall. A well-known news anchor approached Aseem, calling him 'the hero of Cambodia'. Aseem's chest puffed up with pride but Atul intervened to deflate it.

'Don't pump his already inflated ego, he's convinced he's the next big star.'

The news anchor shook Aseem's hand before going his way.

'Now that you're so famous, at least stop harassing me for money.' Atul teased.

Aseem grinned. 'You don't worry about that anymore. I have got an investor.'

The alarm on everyone's faces was priceless. Well, except for Soni—she just smiled, already in on his latest scheme.

'Our future jiju not only has a lot of money but also very astute business sense.' Aseem clarified.

'You didn't!' Radhika had returned, catching the tail end of the conversation.

'He did,' Soni laughed. 'As soon as you introduced him to Jayesh Jiju.'

The moment was interrupted by commotion from inside. Mr Gupta stood red-faced, clutching a letter, barking into his phone: 'What do you mean he's heading to the airport? Stop him!'

Just then Radhika got a message from Jayesh. She broke into a smile as she read it. 'He did it,' she whispered. 'He finally did it.'

She turned to her family. 'Let's go. Our work is done here,' she said. Everyone stood in confusion for a moment. But Radhika repeated it with such conviction and happiness that everyone followed her.

As they piled into the Innova Jayesh had arranged for them, Soni couldn't resist: 'Poor Aseem. He has to find a new investor.' Everyone laughed and the warmth of family filled the car.

Anand, who was always sceptical about Radhika and Jayesh's match, felt an inexplicable sense of relief. He looked back from the front seat.

'Radhu . . . I didn't understand what happened but . . .'

'I am okay, papa. Actually, better than okay, I am happy,' Radhika said.

There was a moment of quiet as their car sped towards the famous temple on the Chhatarpur-Mehrauli road. Until Aseem broke the silence with his latest brainwave.

'I am going to start a podcast.'

The unanimous 'NO!' from everyone made him laugh. Some things would never change, and maybe that wasn't such a bad thing.

Acknowledgements

I didn't plan to be a novelist. Then again—I didn't plan to be a journalist or a film-maker either.

When I started writing this book in 2024, some of my other stories were at various stages of being pitched for movies and shows—a process whose timeline a writer has little control over. I didn't want to add one more story I deeply cared about into that uncertain pipeline. That's when I thought of telling it as a novel. And I'm so glad I did.

This book then, in many ways, is a product of where I am in life—in terms of experience and the people I've been fortunate enough to know or cross paths with. That's why, I'm grateful to all the people I've worked with—my seniors, peers and teammates. Each one of you has shaped me in some way.

I would like to especially thank Mr Uday Shankar—many of my leaps into the unknown were made possible by the quiet confidence I had in him. I would tell myself: If things go really bad, Uday *hain na*. Thank you, sir, for giving me that confidence.

I am deeply thankful to Satya Vyas—the first person to read the complete manuscript—for his inputs, encouragement and for connecting me to Vineet Gill at Penguin Random House India.

To my son Nimish, for finding the name that finally felt right, and for giving me the first set of edit notes.

To my wife Vinti, who always finds ways to keep me working and is the happiest when I manage to do something. Her cheers are the loudest at my smallest wins.

To Vineet Gill, for generously sharing the pitch note and sample chapters with my editor, Deepthi Talwar. And to Deepthi—for her support, clarity and patience in answering all my beginner questions. Having worked in the TV and film industry for years, I'm used to long feedback notes. Deepthi's were like a pleasant gift: simple, effective and encouraging.

To Sparsh Raj Singh and the design team at PRH India, for patiently offering options and incorporating suggestions until we arrived at the cover that's in your hands.

To Areeb Ahmad, for correcting my mistakes and making sure every word landed in the right place. Any that remain are mine alone.

I am also deeply thankful to Arif Ali, Anu Singh Chowdhary, Kamaljeet Negi, Rakesh Kayasth, Sushant Jha and Vivek Anchalia for reading the early chapters and sharing their suggestions.

I am grateful to Anukrti Upadhyay for her generosity in trying to help find representation for the book.

ACKNOWLEDGEMENTS

To Divya Prakash Dubey and Pankaj Dubey, for sharing their experiences as authors and for always being available to answer my questions.

To Mohan Sanda, my go-to friend for anything related to design.

To Manisha Tripathi, Rukmini, Danny, Pori, Shweta, Vibha and Jaspinder—thank you for your constant support during the time I was writing this book.

To my dear friend Vishakh, who helped me find my first two jobs. I don't know what line of work I'd be in today otherwise.

I will always remain indebted to Kirori Mal College. The years I spent in its hostel and on the Delhi University campus are easily the single biggest reason for whatever I have done with my life. Coming from a very protected family environment into that kind of freedom, I did what most good boys—and girls, I think—do. I went a little crazy and experienced life. Those experiences, and the friendships I made along the way, remain my greatest treasure.

To my sister and brother, my sister-in-law and brother-in-law, my nephews and nieces, and my family on Vinti's side—your affection and belief in me mean more than you know.

And finally, to my parents—I can imagine how happy you both would have been, holding this book in your hands. I wish . . . I truly can't put it in words. Thank you for bearing with me, always.

My thanks to all who helped this story find its shape and its way into the world.

Scan QR code to access the
Penguin Random House India website